# "What Did You Do?" Kaitlyn Gasped, Pulling the Blindfold Away.

"Just put some goop on for another electrode," Joyce said.

"Over your third eye," Marisol added stonily.

Joyce cast a sharp, disapproving look at the olive-skinned research assistant. Kaitlyn stared too. But Marisol's face was expressionless.

"What's a third eye?" Kait asked.

"According to legend, it's the seat of all psychic power," Joyce said lightly. "It's in the center of your forehead, where the pineal gland is."

Joyce changed the subject, but Kait was disturbed. Disturbed by the look Joyce gave Marisol, and by the sudden rush of images into her own brain. Kait knew it *wasn't* an electrode touching her forehead. But what else could affect her with such a deep, disturbing power?

*And why was Marisol missing the next day . . . ?*

Books by L. J. Smith

THE FORBIDDEN GAME, VOLUME I: THE HUNTER
THE FORBIDDEN GAME, VOLUME II: THE CHASE
THE FORBIDDEN GAME, VOLUME III: THE KILL
DARK VISIONS, VOLUME I: THE STRANGE POWER

Available from ARCHWAY Paperbacks

# DARK VISIONS

### Volume I

## THE STRANGE POWER

# L.J. SMITH

**AN ARCHWAY PAPERBACK**
Published by POCKET BOOKS
New York   London   Toronto   Sydney   Tokyo   Singapore

This book is a work of fiction. Names, characters, places and
incidents are products of the author's imagination or are used
fictitiously. Any resemblance to actual events or locales or persons,
living or dead, is entirely coincidental.

AN ARCHWAY PAPERBACK *Original*

An Archway Paperback published by
POCKET BOOKS, a division of Simon & Schuster Inc.
1230 Avenue of the Americas, New York, NY 10020

ISBN: 0-671-87454-3

First Archway Paperback printing December 1994

10  9  8  7  6  5  4  3  2  1

AN ARCHWAY PAPERBACK and colophon are
registered trademarks of Simon & Schuster Inc.

Cover art by Danilo Ducak

Printed in the U.S.A.

IL 7+

*For Max, who brought sunshine*

# 1

**Y**ou don't invite the local witch to parties. No matter how beautiful she is. That was the basic problem.

*I don't care,* Kaitlyn thought. *I don't need anyone.*

She was sitting in history class, listening to Marcy Huang and Pam Sasseen plan a party for that weekend. She couldn't help but hear them: Mr. Flynn's gentle, apologetic voice was no competition for their excited whispers. Kait was listening, pretending not to listen, and fiercely wishing she could get away. She couldn't, so she doodled on the blue-lined page of her history notebook.

She was full of contradictory feelings. She hated Pam and Marcy, and wanted them to die, or at least to have some gory accident that left them utterly broken and defeated and miserable. At the same time there was a terrible longing inside her. If they would only let her *in*—it wasn't as if she insisted on being the most popular, the most admired, girl at school. She'd settle

1

for a place in the group that was securely her own. They could shake their heads and say, "Oh, that Kaitlyn—she's odd, but what would we do without her?" And that would be fine, as long as she was a *part*.

But it wouldn't happen, ever. Marcy would never think of inviting Kaitlyn to her party because she wouldn't think of doing something that had never been done before. No one ever invited the witch; no one thought that Kaitlyn, the lovely, spooky girl with the strange eyes, would *want* to go.

And I don't care, Kaitlyn thought, her reflections coming around full circle. This is my last year. One semester to go. After that, I'm out of high school and I hope I never see anyone from this place again.

But that was the other problem, of course. In a little town like Thoroughfare she was bound to see them, and their parents, every day for the next year. And the year after that, and the year after that. . . .

There was no escape. If she could have gone away to college, it might have been different. But she'd screwed up her art scholarship . . . and anyway, there was her father. He needed her—and there wasn't any money. Dad needed her. It was junior college or nothing.

The years stretched out in front of Kaitlyn, bleak as the Ohio winter outside the window, filled with endless cold classrooms. Endless sitting and listening to girls planning parties that she wasn't invited to. Endless exclusion. Endless aching and wishing that she *were* a witch so she could put the most hideous, painful, debilitating curse on all of them.

All the while she was thinking, she was doodling. Or rather her hand was doodling—her brain didn't seem to be involved at all. Now she looked down and for the first time saw what she'd drawn.

A spiderweb.

But what was strange was what was *underneath* the web, so close it was almost touching. A pair of eyes.

Wide, round, heavy-lashed eyes. Bambi eyes. The eyes of a child.

As Kaitlyn stared at it, she suddenly felt dizzy, as if she were falling. As if the picture were opening to let her in. It was a horrible sensation—and a familiar one. It happened every time she drew one of *those* pictures, the kind they called her a witch for.

The kind that came true.

She pulled herself back with a jerk. There was a sick, sinking feeling inside her.

Oh, *please,* no, she thought. Not today—and not here, not at school. It's just a doodle; it doesn't mean anything.

*Please let it be just a doodle.*

But she could feel her body bracing, ignoring her mind, going ice-cold in order to meet what was coming.

A child. She'd drawn a child's eyes, so some child was in danger.

But *what* child? Staring at the space under the eyes, Kait felt a tugging, almost a twitch, in her hand. Her fingers telling her the shape that *needed* to go there. Little half circle, with smaller curves at the edges. A snub nose. Large circle, filled in solid. A mouth, open in fear or surprise or pain. Big curve to indicate a round chin.

A series of long wriggles for hair—and then the itch, the urge, the *need* in Kait's hand ebbed away.

She let out her breath.

That was all. The child in the picture must be a girl, with all that hair. Wavy hair. A pretty little girl with wavy hair and a spiderweb on top of her face.

Something was going to happen, involving a child and a spider. But where—and to what child? And *when?*

Today? Next week? Next year?

It wasn't enough.

It never was. That was the most terrible part of Kaitlyn's terrible gift. Her drawings were always accurate—they always, always came true. She always ended up seeing in real life what she'd drawn on paper.

*But not in time.*

Right now, what could she do? Run through town with a megaphone telling all kids to beware of spiders? Go down to the elementary school looking for girls with wavy hair?

Even if she tried to tell them, they'd run away from her. As if Kaitlyn brought on the things she drew. As if she *made* them happen instead of just predicting them.

The lines of the picture were getting crooked. Kaitlyn blinked to straighten them. The one thing she wouldn't do was cry—because Kaitlyn never cried.

Never. Not once, not since her mother had died when Kait was eight. Since then, Kait had learned how to make the tears go inside.

There was a disturbance at the front of the room. Mr. Flynn's voice, usually so soft and melodious that students could comfortably go to sleep to it, had stopped.

4

Chris Barnable, a boy who worked sixth period as a student aide, had brought a piece of pink paper. A call slip.

Kaitlyn watched Mr. Flynn take it, read it, then look mildly at the class, wrinkling his nose to push his glasses back up.

"Kaitlyn, the office wants you."

Kaitlyn was already reaching for her books. She kept her back very straight, her head very high, as she walked up the aisle to take the slip. KAITLYN FAIRCHILD TO THE PRINCIPAL'S OFFICE—AT ONCE! it read. Somehow when the "at once" box was checked, the whole slip assumed an air of urgency and malice.

"In trouble again?" a voice from the first row asked snidely. Kaitlyn couldn't tell who it was, and she wouldn't turn around to look. She went out the door with Chris.

In trouble again, yes, she thought as she walked down the stairs to the main office. What did they have on her this time? Those excuses "signed by her father" last fall?

Kaitlyn missed a lot of school, because there were times when she just couldn't stand it. Whenever it got too bad, she went down Piqua Road to where the farms were, and drew. Nobody bothered her there.

"I'm sorry you're in trouble," Chris Barnable said as they reached the office. "I mean . . . I'm sorry *if* you're in trouble."

Kaitlyn glanced at him sharply. He was an okay-looking guy: shiny hair, soft eyes—a lot like Hello Sailor, the cocker spaniel she'd had years ago. Still, she wasn't fooled for a minute.

Boys—boys were no good. Kait knew exactly why

they were nice to her. She'd inherited her mother's creamy Irish skin and autumn-fire hair. She'd inherited her mother's supple, willow-slim figure.

But her eyes were her own, and just now she used them without mercy. She turned an icy gaze on Chris, looking at him in a way she was usually careful to avoid. She looked him straight in the face.

He went white.

It was typical of the way people around here reacted when they had to meet Kaitlyn's eyes. No one else had eyes like Kaitlyn. They were smoky blue, and at the outside of each iris, as well as in the middle, were darker rings.

Her father said they were beautiful and that Kaitlyn had been marked by the fairies. But other people said other things. Ever since she could remember, Kaitlyn had heard the whispers—that she had strange eyes, evil eyes. Eyes that saw what wasn't meant to be seen.

Sometimes, like now, Kaitlyn used them as a weapon. She stared at Chris Barnable until the poor jerk actually stepped backward. Then she lowered her lashes demurely and walked into the office.

It gave her only a sick, momentary feeling of triumph. Scaring cocker spaniels was hardly an achievement. But Kaitlyn was too frightened and miserable herself to care. A secretary waved her toward the principal's office, and Kaitlyn steeled herself. She opened the door.

Ms. McCasslan, the principal, was there—but she wasn't alone. Sitting beside the desk was a tanned, trim young woman with short blond hair.

"Congratulations," the blond woman said, coming out of the chair with one quick, graceful movement.

Kaitlyn stood motionless, head high. She didn't know what to think. But all at once she had a rush of feeling, like a premonition.

*This is it. What you've been waiting for.*

She hadn't known she was waiting for anything.

*Of course you have. And this is it.*

*The next few minutes are going to change your life.*

"I'm Joyce," the blond woman said. "Joyce Piper. Don't you remember me?"

# 2

The woman did seem familiar. Her sleek blond hair clung to her head like a wet seal's fur, and her eyes were a startling aquamarine. She was wearing a smart rose-colored suit, but she moved like an aerobics teacher.

Memory burst on Kaitlyn. "The vision screening!"

Joyce nodded. "Exactly!" she said energetically. "Now, how much do you remember about that?"

Bewildered, Kaitlyn looked at Ms. McCasslan. The principal, a small woman, quite plump and very pretty, was sitting with her hands folded on the desk. She seemed serene, but her eyes were sparkling.

All right, so I'm not in trouble, Kait thought. But what's going *on?* She stood uncertainly in the center of the room.

"Don't be frightened, Kaitlyn," the principal said. She waved a small hand with a number of rings on it. "Sit down."

Kait sat.

"I don't bite," Joyce added, sitting down herself, although she kept her aquamarine eyes on Kait's face the entire time. "Now, what do you remember?"

"It was just a test, like you get at the optometrist's," Kaitlyn said slowly. "I thought it was some new program."

Everyone brought their new programs to Ohio. Ohio was so representative of the nation that its people were perfect guinea pigs.

Joyce was smiling a little. "It *was* a new program. But we weren't screening for vision, exactly. Do you remember the test where you had to write down the letters you saw?"

"Oh—yes." It wasn't easy to remember, because everything that had happened during the testing was vague. It had been last fall, early October, Kait thought. Joyce had come into study hall and talked to the class. That was clear enough—Kait remembered her asking them to cooperate. Then Joyce had guided them through some "relaxation exercises"—after which Kaitlyn had been so relaxed that everything was foggy.

"You gave everybody a pencil and a piece of paper," she said hesitantly to Joyce. "And then you projected letters on the movie screen. And they kept getting smaller and smaller. I could hardly write," she added. "I was *limp.*"

"Just a little hypnosis to get past your inhibitions," Joyce said, leaning forward. "What else?"

"I kept writing letters."

"Yes, you did," Joyce said. A slight grin flashed in her tanned face. "You did indeed."

9

After a moment, Kaitlyn said, "So I've got good eyesight?"

"I wouldn't know." Still grinning, Joyce straightened up. "You want to know how that test really worked, Kaitlyn? We kept projecting the letters smaller and smaller—until finally they weren't there at all."

"Weren't there?"

"Not for the last twenty frames. There were just dots, absolutely featureless. You could have vision like a hawk and still not make anything out of them."

A cold finger seemed to run up Kaitlyn's backbone. "I saw letters," she insisted.

"I know you did. But not with your eyes."

There was perfect silence in the room.

Kaitlyn's heart was beating hard.

"We had someone in the room next door," Joyce said. "A graduate student with very good concentration, and *he* was looking at charts with letters on them. That was why you saw letters, Kait. You saw through his eyes. You expected to see letters on the chart, so your mind was open—and you received what he saw."

Kaitlyn said faintly, "It doesn't work that way." Oh, *please,* God . . . all she needed was another power, another curse.

"It does; it's all the same," Joyce said. "It's called remote viewing. The awareness of an event beyond the range of your ordinary senses. Your drawings are remote viewings of events—sometimes events that haven't happened yet."

"What do you know about my drawings?" A rush of emotion brought Kait to her feet. It wasn't fair: this

10

*stranger* coming in and playing with her, testing her, tricking her—and now talking about her private drawings. Her very private drawings that people in Thoroughfare had the decency to only refer to obliquely.

"I'll tell you what I know," Joyce said. Her voice was soft, rhythmic, and she was gazing at Kaitlyn intently with those aquamarine eyes. "I know that you first discovered your gift when you were nine years old. A little boy from your neighborhood had disappeared—"

"Danny Lindenmayer," the principal put in briskly.

"Danny Lindenmayer had disappeared," Joyce said, without looking away from Kait. "And the police were going door to door, looking for him. You were drawing with crayons while they talked to your father. You heard everything about the missing boy. And when you were done drawing, it was a picture you didn't understand, a picture of trees and a bridge . . . and something square."

Kaitlyn nodded, feeling oddly defeated. The memory sucked at her, making her dizzy. That first picture, so dark and strange, and her own fear . . . She'd *known* it was a very bad thing that her fingers had drawn. But she hadn't known why.

"And the next day, on TV, you saw the place where they'd found the little boy's body," Joyce said. "Underneath a bridge by some trees . . . in a packing crate."

"Something square," Kaitlyn said.

"It matched the picture you'd drawn exactly, even though there was no way you could have known about that place. The bridge was thirty miles away, in a town you'd never been to. When your father saw the news on TV, he recognized your picture, too—and he got excited. Started showing the drawing around, telling the story. But people reacted badly. They already thought you were a little different because of your eyes. But this—this was a whole lot different. They didn't like it. And when it happened again, and again, when your drawings kept coming true, they got very frightened."

"And Kaitlyn developed something of an attitude problem," the principal interjected delicately. "She's naturally rebellious and a bit high-strung—like a colt. But she got prickly, too, and cool. Self-defense." She made *tsk*ing noises.

Kaitlyn glared, but it was a feeble glare. Joyce's quiet, sympathetic voice had disarmed her. She sat down again.

"So you know all about me," she said to Joyce. "So I've got an attitude problem. So wh—"

"You do *not* have an attitude problem," Joyce interrupted. She looked almost shocked. She leaned forward, speaking very earnestly. "You have a gift, a very great gift. Kaitlyn, don't you understand? Don't you realize how unusual you are, how wonderful?"

In Kaitlyn's experience, unusual did not equate to wonderful.

"In the entire world, there are only a handful of people who can do what you can do," Joyce said. "In the entire United States, we only found five."

"Five what?"

"Five high school seniors. Five kids like you. All with different talents, of course; none of you can do the same thing. But that's great; that's just what we were looking for. We'll be able to do a variety of experiments."

"You want to *experiment* on me?" Kaitlyn looked at the principal in alarm.

"I'm getting ahead of myself. Let me explain. I'm from San Carlos, California—"

Well, that explained the tan.

"—and I work for the Zetes Institute. It's a very small laboratory, not at all like SRI or Duke University. It was established last year by a research grant from the Zetes Foundation. Mr. Zetes is—oh, how can I explain *him?* He's an incredible man—he's the chairman of a big corporation in Silicon Valley. But his real interest is in psychic phenomena. Psychic research."

Joyce paused and pushed sleek blond hair off her forehead. Kaitlyn could feel her working up to something big. "He's put up the funds for a very special project, a very *intense* project. It was his idea to do screening at high schools all over the country, looking for seniors with high psychic potential. To find the five or six that were absolutely the top, the cream of the crop, and to bring them to California for a year of testing."

"A *year?*"

"That's the beauty of it, don't you see? Instead of doing a few sporadic tests, we'd do testing daily, on a regular schedule. We'd be able to chart changes in your powers with your biorhythms, with your diet—" Joyce broke off abruptly. Looking at Kait directly, she reached out and took Kait's hands.

"Kaitlyn, let down the walls and just *listen* to me for a minute. Can you do that?"

Kait could feel her hands trembling in the cool

13

grasp of the blond woman's fingers. She swallowed, unable to look away from those aquamarine eyes.

"Kaitlyn, I am not here to hurt you. I admire you tremendously. You have a wonderful gift. I want to study it—I've spent my life preparing to study it. I went to college at Duke—you know, where Rhine did his telepathy experiments. I got my master's degree in parapsychology—I've worked at the Dream Laboratory at Maimonides, and the Mind Science Foundation in San Antonio, and the Engineering Anomalies Research Laboratory at Princeton. And all I've ever wanted is a subject like *you*. Together we can prove that what you do is real. We can get hard, replicable, scientific proof. We can show the world that ESP exists."

She stopped, and Kaitlyn heard the whir of a copier in the outer office.

"There are some benefits for Kaitlyn, too," Ms. McCasslan said. "I think you should explain the terms."

"Oh, yes." Joyce let go of Kaitlyn's hands and picked up a manila folder from the desk. "You'll go to a very good school in San Carlos to finish up your senior year. Meanwhile you'll be living at the Institute with the four other students we've chosen. We'll do testing every afternoon, but it won't take long—just an hour or two a day. And at the end of a year, you'll receive a scholarship to the college of your choice." Joyce opened the folder and handed it to Kaitlyn. "A very generous scholarship."

"A *very* generous scholarship," Ms. McCasslan said.

Kaitlyn found herself looking at a number on a piece of paper. "That's . . . for all of us, to split?"

"That is for you," Joyce said. "Alone."

Kaitlyn felt dizzy.

"You'll be helping the cause of science," Joyce said. "And you could make a new life for yourself. A new start. No one at your new school needs to know why you're there; you can just be an ordinary high school kid. Next fall you can go to Stanford or San Francisco State University—San Carlos is just half an hour south of San Francisco. And after that, you're free. You can go anywhere."

Kaitlyn felt *really* dizzy.

"You'll love the Bay Area. Sunshine, nice beaches— do you realize it was seventy degrees there yesterday when I left? Seventy degrees in winter. Redwoods— palm trees—"

"I can't," Kaitlyn said weakly.

Joyce and the principal both looked at her, startled.

"I can't," Kait said again, more loudly, pulling her walls close around her. She needed the walls, or she might succumb to the shimmering picture Joyce was painting in her mind.

"Don't you want to get away?" Joyce said gently.

Didn't she? Only so much that she sometimes felt like a bird beating its wings against glass. Except that she'd never been quite sure what she'd *do* once she got away. She'd just thought, There must be some place I belong. A place where I'd just fit in, without trying.

She'd never thought of *California* as being the place. California was almost too rich, too heady and exciting. It was like a dream. And the money . . .

But her father.

"You don't understand. It's my dad. I've never been away from him, not since my mom died, and he needs me. He's not . . . He really needs me."

Ms. McCasslan was looking sympathetic. Ms. McCasslan knew her dad, of course. He'd been brilliant, a philosophy professor; he'd written books. But after Kaitlyn's mother had died, he'd gotten . . . vague. Now he sang a lot to himself and did odd jobs around town. He didn't make much doing them. When bills came in, he shuffled his feet and ruffled his hair, looking anxious and ashamed. He was almost like a kid—but he adored Kait and she adored him. She would never let anything hurt him.

And to leave him so soon, before she was even old enough to go to college—and to go all the way to California—and for a *year*—

"It's impossible," she said.

Ms. McCasslan was looking down at her plump hands. "But, Kaitlyn, don't you think he'd want you to go? To do what's best for you?"

Kaitlyn shook her head. She didn't want to listen to arguments. Her mind was made up.

"Wouldn't you like to learn to control your talents?" Joyce said.

Kaitlyn looked at her.

The possibility of control had never occurred to her. The pictures came when she wasn't expecting them; took over her hand without her realizing it. She never knew what had happened until it was over.

"I think you can learn," Joyce said. "I think you and I could learn, together."

Kaitlyn opened her mouth, but before she could answer, there was a terrible sound from outside the office.

It was a crashing and a grinding and a shattering all together. And it was a *huge* noise, so huge that Kaitlyn knew at once it could come from nothing ordinary. It sounded very close.

Joyce and Ms. McCasslan had both jumped up, and it was the plump little principal who made it to the door first. She rushed out through the office to the street, with Kait and Joyce following her.

People were running up on either side of Harding Street, crunching through the snow. Cold air bit Kaitlyn's cheeks. The slanting afternoon sunlight threw up sharp contrasts between light and shadow, making the scene in front of Kaitlyn look frighteningly focused and distinct.

A yellow Neon was facing the wrong way on Harding Street, its back wheels on the sidewalk, its left side a wreck. It looked as if it had been broadsided and spun. Kaitlyn recognized it; it belonged to Jerry Crutchfield, one of the few students who had a car.

In the middle of the street, a dark blue station wagon was facing Kaitlyn directly. Its entire front end was accordioned. The metal was twisted and deformed, the headlights shattered.

Polly Vertanen, a junior, was tugging at Ms. McCasslan's sleeve. "I saw everything, Ms. McCasslan. Jerry just pulled out of the parking lot— but the station wagon was going too fast. They just hit him. . . . I saw everything. They were going too fast."

"That's Marian Günter's station wagon," Ms.

McCasslan said sharply. "That's her little girl in there. Don't move her yet! Don't move her!" The principal's voice went on, but Kait didn't hear any more.

She was staring at the windshield of the station wagon. She hadn't seen before—but she could see now.

People around her were yelling, running. Kaitlyn hardly noticed them. Her entire world was filled with the car windshield.

The little girl had been thrown up against it—or maybe it had crunched back up against her. She was actually lying with her forehead touching the glass, as if she were looking out with open eyes.

With wide eyes. Wide, round, heavy-lashed eyes. Bambi eyes.

She had a small snub nose and a round chin. Wavy blond hair stuck to the glass.

The glass itself was shattered like a spiderweb, a spiderweb superimposed on the child's face.

"Oh, no—please, no . . ." Kaitlyn whispered.

She found herself clutching, without knowing what she was clutching at. Somebody steadied her.

Sirens were wailing closer. A crowd was gathering around the station wagon, blocking Kaitlyn's view of the child.

She knew Curt Günter. The little girl must be Lindy, his baby sister. Why hadn't Kait realized? Why hadn't her picture shown her? Why couldn't it have shown her cars crashing, with a *date* and a *place,* instead of that pathetic kid's face? How could it all be so *useless,* so completely freaking *useless* . . . ?

"Do you need to sit down?" the person holding her asked, and it was Joyce Piper, and she was shivering.

Kait was shivering, too. Her breath was coming very fast. She clutched harder at Joyce.

"Did you mean that, about me learning to control . . . what I do?" Kait couldn't call it a talent.

Joyce looked from her to the accident scene with something like dawning realization. "I think so. I hope so."

"You have to *promise*."

Joyce met her gaze full on, the way people in Thoroughfare never did. "I promise to try, Kait."

"Then I'll go. My dad will understand."

Joyce's aquamarine eyes were brilliant. "I'm so glad." She shivered violently. "Seventy degrees there, Kait," she added softly, almost absently. "Pack light."


That night, Kaitlyn had a strangely realistic dream. She was on a rocky peninsula, a spit of land surrounded by cold gray ocean. The clouds overhead were almost black and the wind blew spray into her face. She could actually feel the wet of it, the chill.

From just behind her, someone called her name. But when she turned, the dream ended.

# 3

**K**ait got off the plane feeling giddy and triumphant. She'd never been on a plane before, but it had been easy as anything. She'd chewed gum on takeoff and landing, done twists in the tiny bathroom every hour to keep limber, and brushed her hair and straightened her red dress as the plane cruised up to the gate. Perfection.

She was very happy. Somehow, once the decision to go was made, Kait's spirits had lifted and lifted. It no longer seemed a grim necessity to come to the Institute; it was the dream Joyce had described, the beginning of a new life. Her dad had been unbelievably sweet and understanding—he'd seen her off just as if she were going to college. Joyce was supposed to meet her here at San Francisco Airport.

But the airport was crowded and there was no sign of Joyce. People streamed by. Kaitlyn stuck close to the gate, head high, trying to look nonchalant. The last thing she wanted was anyone to ask if she needed help.

"Excuse me."

Kaitlyn flicked a sideways glance at the unfamiliar voice. It wasn't help; it was something even more disturbing. One of those cult people who hang around airports and ask for money. He was wearing reddish robes—Tuscan red, Kait thought. If she were going to draw them.

"I'd like a moment of your time, please." The voice was civil, but persistent—authoritative. It sounded foreign.

Kait edged away—or started to. A hand caught her. She looked down at it in amazement, seeing lean fingers the color of caramel locked around her wrist.

*Okay, jerk, you asked for it.* Outraged, Kait turned the full power of her smoky blue, strangely ringed eyes on him.

He just looked back—and when Kait looked deeply into *his* eyes, she reeled.

His skin was that caramel color—but his eyes were slanting and very dark, with an epicanthic fold. The phrase "lynx-eyed" came to Kaitlyn's mind. His softly curling hair was a sort of pale shimmery brown, like silver birch. None of it went together.

But that wasn't what made her reel. It was a feeling of *age* from him. When she looked into his eyes, she had the sense of centuries passing. Millennia. His face was unlined, but there were ice ages in his eyes.

Kait couldn't remember ever really screaming in her life, but she decided to scream now.

She didn't get a chance. The grip on her wrist

tightened and before she could draw a breath, she was jerked off balance, moving. The man in the robes was pulling her backward into the jetway—the long corridor that led to a plane.

Except that there was no plane now and the corridor was empty. The double doors closed, cutting Kaitlyn off from the rest of the airport. She was still too shocked to scream.

"Don't move and you won't get hurt," the man in the robes said grimly. His lynx eyes were hard.

Kaitlyn didn't believe him. He was from some cult and he was obviously insane and he'd dragged her into this deserted place. She should have fought him before; she should have screamed when she had the chance. Now she was trapped.

Without letting go of her arm, the man fumbled inside his robes.

For a gun or a knife, Kaitlyn thought. Her heart was pounding violently. If he would just relax his grip on her arm for an instant—if she could get to the other side of those doors where there were people . . .

"Here," the man said. "All I want is for you to look at this."

He was holding not a weapon but a piece of paper. Glossy paper that had been folded. To Kaitlyn's dazed eyes it looked like a brochure.

I don't believe it, she thought. He *is* insane.

"Just *look*," the man said.

Kaitlyn couldn't help looking; he was holding the paper in her face. It seemed to be a full-color picture of a rose garden. A walled rose garden, with a fountain in the center, and something thrusting out of the fountain. Maybe an ice sculpture, Kaitlyn thought dizzily. It was tall, white, and semitransparent—like a faceted column. In one of its many facets was the tiny, perfect reflection of a rose.

Kaitlyn's heart was still pounding violently. This was all *too* weird. As frightening as if he were trying to hurt her.

"This crystal—" the man began, and then Kaitlyn saw her chance.

The iron grip on her arm loosened just the slightest bit as he spoke, and his eyes were on the picture. Kaitlyn kicked backward, glad that she was wearing pumps with her red dress, slamming a two-inch heel into his shin. The man yelped and let go.

Kaitlyn hit the double doors with both hands, bursting out into the airport, and then she just ran. She ran without looking behind her to see if the man was following. She dodged around chairs and phone booths, heading blindly into the crowd.

She didn't stop until someone called her name.

"Kaitlyn!"

It was Joyce, heading the other way, toward the gate. Kait had never been so relieved to see anyone.

"I'm so sorry—the traffic was terrible—and parking in this place is always—" She broke off. "Kaitlyn, what's wrong?"

Kaitlyn collapsed in Joyce's arms. Now that she was safe, she somehow wanted to laugh. Hysteria, probably, she told herself. Her legs were shaking.

"It was too strange," she gasped. "There was this guy from some cult or something—and he grabbed me. He probably just wanted money, but I thought—"

"He *grabbed* you? Where is he now?"

Kaitlyn waved a hand vaguely. "Back there. I kicked him and ran."

Joyce's aquamarine eyes flashed with grim approval, but all she said was, "Come on. We'd better tell airport security about this."

"Oh—I'm okay now. He was just some nut. . . ."

"Nuts like that, we put away. Even in California," Joyce said flatly.

Airport security sent people looking for the man, but he was gone.

"Besides," the guard told Joyce and Kaitlyn, "he *couldn't* have opened the doors to the jet bridge. They're kept locked."

Kaitlyn didn't want to argue. She wanted to forget all about it and go to the Institute. This was *not* how she'd planned her grand entrance to California.

"Let's go," she said to Joyce, and Joyce sighed and nodded.

They picked up Kaitlyn's luggage and carried it to a sharp little green convertible—Joyce's car. Kait felt like bouncing on the seat as Joyce drove. Back home it was freezing, with twenty inches of snow on the ground. Here they drove with the top down, and Joyce's blond hair ruffled like down in the wind.

"How's the little girl from the crash?" Joyce asked.

Kaitlyn's spirits pitched.

"She's still in the hospital. They don't know if she'll be okay." Kaitlyn clamped her lips together to show that she didn't intend to answer any more questions about Lindy.

But Joyce didn't ask any more questions. Instead, she said, "Two of your housemates are already at the Institute; Lewis and Anna. I think you'll like them."

Lewis—a boy. "How many of the five of us are boys?" Kaitlyn asked suspiciously.

"Three, I'm afraid," Joyce said gravely, and then gave Kait a sideways look of amusement.

Kaitlyn declined to be amused. Three boys and only one other girl. Three sloppy, meaty-handed, too-big-to-control, hormone-crazed Power Rangers.

Kaitlyn had tried boys once, two years ago when she was a sophomore. She'd let one of them take her out, driving up to Lake Erie every Friday and Saturday night, and she'd put up with what he wanted—*some* of what he wanted—while he talked about Metallica and the Browns and the Bengals and his candy-apple-red Trans Am. All of which Kait knew nothing about. After the first date, she decided that guys must be an alien species, and just tried to deal with him without listening to him. She was still hoping that he'd take her to the next party with his crowd.

She had it all planned out. He'd escort her into one of those big houses on the hill that she'd never been invited to. She'd wear something a little dowdy so as to not show up the hostess. With her boyfriend's arm around her shoulder, she'd be modest and self-effacing, complimenting everything in sight. The whole crowd would see she wasn't a monster. They'd let her in—maybe not all at once, but over time, as they got used to her being around.

Wrong.

When she brought up the party, her lake-loving boyfriend blustered around, but eventually the truth came clear. He wasn't going to take her anywhere in public. She was good enough alone in the dark with him, but not good enough to be seen with him in the daylight.

It was one of the times when it was hardest not to cry. Stiff-lipped, she'd ordered him to take her home. He got angrier and angrier as they drove. When she jerked the car door open, he said, "I was going to dump you anyway. You're not like a normal girl. You're *cold.*"

Kait stared after the car when it had gone. So she wasn't normal. Fine, she knew that already. So she was *cold*—and the way he'd said it made it obvious that he didn't just mean her personality. He meant more.

Well, that was fine, too. She'd rather be cold all her life than feel anything with a guy like that. The memory of his humid palms on her arms made her want to wipe her own hands on the skirt of her red dress.

So I'm cold, Kait thought now, shifting in the front seat of Joyce's convertible. So what? There are other things in life to be interested in.

And really, she didn't care how many boys were at the Institute. She'd ignore them—she'd stick with Anna. She just hoped Anna wasn't boy-crazy.

*And that she likes you,* a small, nerve-racking voice in her head added. Kaitlyn squashed the thought, tossing her head to feel the wind snapping her hair back, enjoying the motion and the sunshine.

"Is it much farther?" she asked. "I can't wait."

Joyce laughed. "No, it's not far."

They were driving through residential streets now. Kaitlyn looked around eagerly, but with a tingling in her stomach. What if the Institute was too big, too sterile, too intimidating? She'd pictured a large, squat redbrick building, something like her old high school back in Thoroughfare.

Joyce turned the convertible in to a driveway, and Kait stared.

"Is *this* it?"

"Yup."

"But it's *purple.*"

It was extremely purple. The shingled sides were a cool but vivid purple, the wood trim around the windows was darker purple; the door and wraparound balcony were glaring high-gloss purple. The only things that weren't purple were the slate gray roof and the bricks in the chimney.

Kait felt as if someone had dropped her into a swimming pool full of grape juice. She didn't know if she loved the color scheme or hated it.

"We haven't had time to paint it yet," Joyce explained, parking. "We've been busy converting most of the first floor to labs—but you can have the full tour tomorrow. Why don't you go up and meet your housemates?"

Thrills of nervousness wound through Kait's stomach. The Institute was so much smaller, so much more intimate, than she'd imagined. She'd really be *living* with these people.

"Sure, that's fine," she said, and held her head very high as she got out of the car.

"Don't worry about the luggage yet—just go on in. Go straight past the living room and you'll see a staircase on your right. Take that upstairs—the whole second floor is for you kids. I told Lewis and Anna that you can work out the bedroom situation for yourselves."

Kaitlyn went, trying not to either dawdle or hurry. She wouldn't let anyone see how nervous she was. The very purple front door was unlocked. The inside of the house wasn't purple—it looked quite ordinary, with a large living room on the right and a large enough dining room on the left.

*Don't look at it now. Go on up.*

Kaitlyn's feet carried her down the tiled foyer that separated them, until she reached the staircase.

*Take it slow. Just keep breathing.*

But her heart was going quickly, and her feet wanted to leap up the steps. The stairs made a U-turn at a landing and then she was at the top.

The hallway was crowded with odds and ends of furniture, piled haphazardly. In front of Kait and to the left was an open door. She could hear voices inside.

*Okay, who cares if they're nice? They're probably creeps—and I don't care. I don't need anyone. Maybe I can learn to put curses on people.*

The last-minute panic made her reckless, and she plunged through the door almost belligerently.

And stopped. A girl was kneeling on a bed without sheets or blankets. A lovely girl—graceful and dark, with high cheekbones and an expression of serenity. Kaitlyn's belligerence seeped away and all the walls she normally kept around her seemed to dissolve. Peacefulness seemed to come from the other girl like a cool wind.

The girl smiled. "You're Kaitlyn."

"And you're . . . Anna?"

"Anna Eva Whiteraven."

"What a wonderful name," Kaitlyn said.

It wasn't the sort of thing people said back at Warren G. Harding High School—but Kaitlyn wasn't at Warren G. Harding High School anymore, and Anna's serene expression broke into another smile.

*"You've* got wonderful eyes," she said.

"Does she?" another voice said eagerly. "Hey, turn around."

Kait was already turning. On the far side of the room was an alcove with a bay window—and a boy coming out of it. He didn't look threatening. He had a cap of black hair and dark, almond-shaped eyes. From the camera in his hands Kaitlyn guessed he'd been taking pictures out the open window.

"Smile!" A flashbulb blinded Kaitlyn.

*"Ouch!"*

"Sorry; I just wanted to preserve the moment." The boy let go of the camera, which bounced as the strap around his neck caught it, and stuck out a hand. "You do have kind of neat eyes. Kind of weird. I'm Lewis Chao."

He had a sweet face, Kaitlyn decided. He wasn't big and gross, but rather small and neat. His hand wasn't sweaty when she took it, and his eyes weren't hungry.

"Lewis has been taking pictures since we got here this morning," Anna said. "We've got the entire block on record."

Kaitlyn blinked away blue afterimages and looked at Lewis curiously. "Really? Where do you come from?" It must be even farther away than Ohio, she thought.

He smiled beatifically. "San Francisco."

Kaitlyn laughed, and suddenly they were all laughing together. Not malicious laughter, not laughing *at* anyone, but wonderful torrents of giggles *together*. And then Kait knew.

I'm going to be happy here, she realized. It was almost too big a concept to take in at once. She was going to be happy, and for a year. A panorama opened before her. Sitting by the fireplace she'd seen downstairs, studying, the others all doing their own projects, everyone joined by a warm sort of togetherness even while they did their own things. Each of them different, but not minding the differences.

No need for walls between them.

They began to talk, eagerly, friendship flying back and forth. It seemed quite natural to join Anna sitting on the bed.

"I'm from Ohio—" Kait started.

"Aha, a Buckeye," Lewis put in.

"I'm from Washington State," Anna said. "Near Puget Sound."

"You're Native American, aren't you?"

"Yes; Suquamish."

"She talks to animals," Lewis said.

Anna said gently, "I don't really talk to them. I can influence them to do things—sometimes. It's a kind of thought projection, Joyce says."

*Thought projection with animals?* A few weeks ago Kait would have said it sounded insane—but then, wasn't her own "talent" insane? If one was possible, so was the other.

"I've got PK," Lewis said. "That's psychokinesis. Mind over matter."

"Like . . . spoon bending?" Kait asked uncertainly.

"Nah, spoon bending's a trick. Real PK is only for little things, like making a compass needle deflect. What do you do?"

Despite herself, Kaitlyn's heart bumped. She'd never in her life said aloud the thing she was going to say.

"I . . . kind of see the future. At least, I don't, but my drawings do, and when I look back at them, I see that they did. But usually only after the thing has already happened," she finished incoherently.

Lewis and Anna looked thoughtful. "That's cool," Lewis said at last, and Anna said, "So you're an artist?"

The relief that flooded Kaitlyn was painful, and its aftermath left her jubilant. "I guess. I like to draw."

I'd like to draw right now, she thought, dying to get hold of some pastels. She'd draw Anna with burnt umber and matte black and sienna. She'd do Lewis with blue-black—his hair was that shiny—and some sort of flesh-ocher mixture for his skin.

Later, she told herself. Aloud she said, "So what about the bedrooms up here? Who goes where?"

"That's just what we've been trying to figure out," Anna said. "The problem is that there are supposed to be five of us students, and they've only got four bedrooms. There's this one and another one even bigger next door, and then two smaller ones on the back side of the house."

"And only the big ones have cable hookup. I've explained and explained," said Lewis, looking tragic, "that I *need* my MTV, but she doesn't understand. And I need enough outlets for my computer and stereo and stuff. Only the big rooms have those."

"It's not fair for us to take the good rooms before the others even get here," Anna said, gently but firmly.

"But I *need* my MTV. I'll *die.*"

"Well, I don't care about cable," Kaitlyn said. "But I'd like a room with northern light—I like to draw in the mornings."

"You haven't heard the worst part—all the rooms have different things," Lewis said. "The one next door is *huge,* and it's got a king-size bed and a balcony and a Jacuzzi bath. This one has the alcove over there and a private bathroom—but almost no closet. And the two rooms in back have okay closets, but they share a bathroom."

"Well, obviously the biggest room should go to whoever's rooming together—because two of us are going to *have* to room together," Kaitlyn said.

"Great. I'll room with either of you," Lewis said promptly.

"No, no, no—look, let me go check out the light in the smaller rooms," Kaitlyn said, jumping up.

"Check out the Jacuzzi instead," Lewis called after her.

In the hallway, Kait turned to laugh at him over her shoulder—and ran directly into someone cresting the top of the stairs.

It wasn't a hard knock, but Kaitlyn automatically recoiled, and ran her leg into something hard. Pain flared just behind her knee, rendering her momentarily speechless. She clenched her teeth and glared down at the thing that had hurt her. A nightstand with one sharp-edged drawer pulled out. What was all this furniture *doing* in the hall, anyway?

"I'm really sorry," a soft southern voice drawled. "Are you all right?"

Kaitlyn looked at the tanned, blond boy who'd run into her. It *would* be a boy, of course. And a big one, not small and safe like Lewis. The kind of boy who disturbed the space around him, filling the whole hallway with his presence. A very *masculine* presence —if Anna was a cool wind, this boy was a golden solar flare.

Since ignoring was out of the question, Kaitlyn turned her best glare on him. He returned the look mildly and she realized with a start that his eyes were amber-colored—golden. Just a few shades darker than his hair.

"You *are* hurt," he said, apparently mistaking the glare for suffering. "Where?" Then he did something that dumbfounded Kaitlyn. He dropped to his knees.

He's going to apologize, she thought wildly. Oh, God, everyone in California *is* nuts.

But the boy didn't apologize—he didn't even look up at her. He was reaching for her leg.

"This one here, right?" he said in that southern-gentleman voice.

Kaitlyn's mouth opened, but all she could do was stare at him. She was backed against the wall—there was nowhere to escape.

"Back here—this spot?" And then, deftly and unceremoniously, he turned up the skirt of her red dress. Kaitlyn's mind went into shock. She simply had no experience that had prepared her to deal with this situation—a perfect stranger reaching under her dress in a public place. And it was the *way* he did it; not like

33

a grabby boy at all, but like . . . like . . . a doctor examining a patient.

"It's not a cut. Just a knot," the boy said. He wasn't looking at her or the leg, but down the hallway. His fingers were running lightly over the painful area, as if assessing it. They felt dry but warm—unnaturally warm.

"You'll have a bad bruise if you leave it, though. Why don't you hold still and let me see if I can help?"

This, at last, catapulted Kait out of silence.

"Hold *still? Hold still for what . . . ?*"

He waved a hand. "Be quiet, now—please."

Kaitlyn was stupefied.

"Yes," the boy said, as if to himself. "I think I can help this some. I'll try."

Kaitlyn held still because she was paralyzed. She could feel his fingers on the back of her knee—a terribly intimate place, extremely tender and vulnerable. Kait couldn't remember *anyone* touching her there, not even her doctor.

Then the touch changed. It became a burning, tingling feeling. Like slow fire. It was almost like pain, but—

Kait gasped. "What are you *doing* to me? Stop that—what are you *doing?*"

He spoke in a soft, measured voice, without glancing up. "Channeling energy. Trying."

"I said *stop*—oh."

"Work with me, now, please. Don't fight me."

Kaitlyn just stared down at the top of his head. His gold-blond hair was unruly, springing in curls and waves.

A strange sensation swept through Kait, flowing up from her knee and through her body, branching out to every blood vessel and capillary. A feeling of refreshment—of *renewal*. It was like getting a drink of clean, cold water when you were desperately thirsty, or being drenched with delicious icy mist when you were hot. Kaitlyn suddenly felt that until this moment, she had only been half-awake.

The boy was making odd motions now, as if he were brushing lint off the back of her knee. Touch, shake off. Touch, shake off. As if gathering something and then shaking drops of water off his fingers.

Kaitlyn suddenly realized that her pain was completely gone.

"That's it," the boy said cheerfully. "Now if I can just close this off . . ." He cupped a warm hand around the back of her knee. "There. It shouldn't bruise now."

The boy stood up briskly and brushed off his hands. He was breathing as if he'd just run a race.

Kaitlyn stared at him. She herself felt *ready* to run a race. She had never felt so refreshed—so alive. At the same time, as she got another glimpse of his face, she thought maybe she ought to sit down.

When he looked back at her, she expected . . . well, she didn't know what. But what she *didn't* expect was a quick, almost absentminded smile from a boy who was already turning around to leave.

"Sorry about that. Guess I'd better go down and help Joyce with the luggage—before I knock anyone else over." He started down the stairs.

*"Wait* a minute—who are you? And—"

"Rob." He smiled over his shoulder. "Rob Kessler." He reached the landing, turned, and was gone.

"—and how did you *do* that?" Kait demanded of empty air.

Rob. Rob Kessler, she thought.

"Hey, Kaitlyn!" It was Lewis's voice from the bedroom. "Are you out there? Hey, Kaitlyn, come quick!"

# 4

**K**aitlyn hesitated, still looking down the stairs. Then she gathered her self-possession and slowly walked back into the room. Lewis and Anna were in the alcove, looking out the window.

"He's here," Lewis said excitedly, and brought his camera up. "That's got to be him!"

*"Who's* here?" Kaitlyn asked, hoping no one would look at her too closely. She felt flushed.

"Mr. Zetes," said Lewis. "Joyce said he had a limo."

A black limousine was parked outside the house, one of its rear doors open. A white-haired man stood beside the door, dressed in a greatcoat which Kaitlyn thought must be terribly hot on this Californian afternoon. He had a gold-topped cane—a real gold-topped cane, Kaitlyn thought in fascination.

"Looks like he's brought some friends," Anna said, smiling. Two large black dogs were jumping out of the limo. They started for the bushes but came back at a word from the man and stood on either side of him.

"Cute," Kaitlyn said. "But what's *that?*" A white van was turning in the driveway. Lettering on its side read DEPARTMENT OF YOUTH AUTHORITY.

Lewis brought his camera down, looking awed. "Jeez. That's the California Youth Authority."

"Which is . . . ?"

"It's the last stop. It's where they put the *baaaaad* boys. The hard-core kids who can't make it at any of the regular juvie places."

Anna's quiet voice said, "You mean it's jail?"

"My dad says it's the place for kids who're on their way to state prison. You know, the murderers and stuff."

*"Murderers?"* Kait exclaimed. "Well, what's it doing here, then? You don't think . . ." She looked at Anna, who looked back, serenity a bit clouded. Clearly, Anna did think.

They both looked at Lewis, whose almond-shaped eyes were wide.

"I think we'd better get down there," Kaitlyn said.

They hurried downstairs, bursting out onto the wooden porch and trying to look inconspicuous. No one was looking at them, anyway. Mr. Zetes was talking to a khaki-uniformed officer standing by the van.

Kaitlyn could only catch a few words of what was said—"Judge Baldwin's authority" and "CYA ward" and "rehabilitation."

". . . your responsibility," the officer finished, and stepped away from the van's door.

A boy came out. Kaitlyn could feel her eyebrows go up.

He was startlingly handsome—but there was a cold wariness in his face and movements. His hair and eyes were dark, but his skin was rather pale. One of the few people in California without a tan, Kaitlyn thought.

*"Chiaroscuro,"* she murmured.

"What?" Lewis whispered.

"It's an art word. It means 'light and shade'—like in a drawing where you only use black and white." As Kaitlyn finished, she suddenly felt herself shiver. There was something strange about this boy, as if—as if—

As if he weren't quite canny, her mind supplied. At least, that's the phrase people back home used to use about *you,* isn't it?

The van was driving off. Mr. Zetes and the dark-haired boy were walking up to the door.

"Looks like we've got a new housemate," Lewis said under his breath. "Oh, boy."

Mr. Zetes gave a courtly nod to the group on the porch. "I see you're here. I believe everyone has arrived now—if you'll come inside, we can commence with the introductions." He went in, and the two dogs followed him. They were rottweilers, Kaitlyn noted, and rather fierce-looking.

Anna and Lewis stepped back silently as the new boy approached, but Kaitlyn held her ground. She knew what it was like to have people step back when you walked near them. The boy passed very close to her, and turned to give her a direct look as he did. Kaitlyn saw that his eyes weren't black, but a very dark gray. She had the distinct feeling that he wanted to unsettle her, to make her look down.

I wonder what he did to get in prison, she thought, feeling chilled again. She followed the others into the house.

"Mr. Zetes!" Joyce said happily from the living room. She caught the old man's arm, smiling and gesturing with enthusiasm as she spoke to him.

Kait's attention was caught by a blond head near the stairs. Rob Kessler had a duffel bag—*her* duffel bag—slung over his shoulder. He saw the group that had just come in, and started toward them . . . and then he stopped.

His entire body had stiffened. Kaitlyn followed his gaze down the foyer—to the new boy.

Who was equally stiff. His dark gray eyes were fixed on Rob with complete attention and icy hatred. His body was held as if ready for an attack as Rob came closer.

One of the two rottweilers by Mr. Zetes began to growl.

"Good dog, Carl," Lewis said nervously.

*"You,"* the new boy said to Rob.

*"You,"* Rob said to the new boy.

"You two know each other?" Kaitlyn said to both of them.

Rob spoke without looking away from the other boy's pale, wary face. "From a ways back," he said. He let the duffel bag down with a thump.

"Not a long enough ways," the other boy said. In contrast to Rob's soft southern tones, his voice was harsh and clipped.

Both dogs were growling now.

Well, there goes any chance of harmony between housemates, Kaitlyn thought. She noticed that Mr. Zetes and Joyce had broken off talking and were looking at the students.

"We all seem to be together," Mr. Zetes said rather dryly, and Joyce said, "Come over here, everybody! This is the moment I've been waiting for."

Rob and the new boy slowly turned away from each other. Joyce gave the group a brilliant smile as they gathered around. Her aquamarine eyes were sparkling.

"Kids, it's an honor and a privilege to introduce you to the man who brought you all here—the man who's responsible for this project. This is Mr. Zetes."

Kaitlyn felt for a moment as if she ought to applaud. Instead, she murmured "Hello" with the others. Mr. Zetes bent his head in recognition, and Joyce went on.

"Mr. Zetes, these are the troops. Anna Whiteraven, from Washington." The old man shook hands with her, and with each of them as Joyce introduced them. "Lewis Chao from California. Kaitlyn Fairchild from Ohio. Rob Kessler from North Carolina. And Gabriel Wolfe from . . . here and there."

"Yeah, depending on where the charges are pending," Rob drawled, not quite aloud. Mr. Zetes gave him a piercing look.

"Gabriel has been released into my custody," he said. "His parole allows him to go to school; for the rest of the time, he's confined to this house. He knows what will happen if he tries to violate those conditions —don't you, Gabriel?"

Gabriel's dark gray eyes moved from Rob to Mr. Zetes. He said one word, expressionlessly. "Yes."

"Good." Mr. Zetes looked at the rest of the group. "While you're here, I expect you all to try to get along. I don't think any of you can realize, at your age, just how great a gift has been given to you. Your one job here is to see that you *use* that gift wisely, and make the most of it."

Now for the pep talk, Kait thought, studying Mr. Zetes. He had an impressive shock of white hair on his handsome old head and a broad and benevolent brow. Kaitlyn thought suddenly, *I* know what he looks like. He looks like Little Lord Fauntleroy's grandfather, the earl.

But the earl wasn't giving any ordinary pep talk. "One thing you need to realize from the start is that you're different from the rest of humanity. You've been . . . chosen. Branded. You'll never be like other people, so there's no reason even to try. You follow different laws."

Kaitlyn felt her eyebrows pull together. Joyce had said similar things, but somehow Mr. Zetes's words had another tone. She wasn't sure she liked it.

"You have something inside you that won't be repressed. A hidden power that burns like a flame," he went on. "You're *superior* to the rest of humanity— don't ever forget that."

Is he trying to flatter us? Kait wondered. Because if he is, it isn't working. It all sounds . . . hollow, somehow.

"You are the pioneers in an exploration that has infinite possibilities. The work you do here may change the way the entire world looks at psychic powers—it may change the way the human race looks at itself. You young people are actually in a position to benefit all humankind."

Suddenly Kait felt the need to draw.

Not the ordinary need, like the desire she'd had to draw Lewis and Anna. This was the need that came with an itch in her hand—and the internal shiver that meant a premonition.

But she couldn't just walk away while Mr. Zetes was talking. She glanced around the room in distraction—and met Gabriel's eyes.

Right now those eyes looked dark and wicked, as if something in Mr. Zetes's speech amused him. Amused him in a cynical way.

With a shock, Kaitlyn realized that he looked as if he also found Mr. Zetes's words hollow. And the way he was gazing at her seemed to show that he knew she did, too.

Kaitlyn felt herself flushing. She looked quickly back at Mr. Zetes, freezing her face into an interested, deferential expression. After all, he was the one paying her scholarship. He might be a little eccentric, but he obviously had a good heart.

By the time the speech was over, her need to draw was gone.

After Mr. Zetes was finished, Joyce said a few words about how she wanted them to do their best in the next year. "I'll be living at the Institute with you," she added. "My room is back there"—she pointed to a set of French doors beyond the living room that looked as if they led outside—"and you can feel free to come to me at any time, day or night. Oh, and here's someone else you'll be working with."

Kaitlyn turned and saw a girl coming through the dining room. She looked college age, and had tumbled mahogany hair and full lips which looked a bit sullen.

"This is Marisol Diaz, an undergrad from Stanford," Joyce said. "She won't live here, but she'll come daily and help with your testing. She'll also help me cook. You'll find a schedule for meals on the dining room wall, and we'll go over the other house rules tomorrow. Any questions?"

Heads were shaken.

"Good. Now, why don't you go upstairs and fix up your rooms? It's been a long day, and I know some of you must be tired from jet lag. Marisol and I will throw together something for dinner."

Kaitlyn *was* tired. Although her watch said 5:45, it was three hours later by Ohio time. Mr. Zetes said good-bye to each of them, and shook their hands. Then Kait and the others headed upstairs.

"What did you think of him?" she whispered to Lewis and Anna as they reached the second floor.

"Impressive—but a little scary. I kept expecting him to introduce 'Masterpiece Theater,'" Lewis whispered back.

"Those dogs were interesting," Anna said. "Usually I can sort of read animals, tell if they're happy or sad or whatever. But those two were very guarded. I wouldn't want to try to influence them."

Something made Kait glance behind her—and she found that Gabriel was looking at her. She felt disconcerted, so she immediately went on the attack.

"And what did *you* think?" she asked him.

"I think he wants to use us for his own reasons."

"Use us how?" Kaitlyn said sharply.

Gabriel shrugged, looking bored. "How should I know? Maybe to improve his corporation's image— 'Silicon Valley Company Benefits Humankind.' Like Chevron financing wildlife programs. Of course, he was right about one thing—we *are* superior to the rest of the human race."

"And some of us are more superior than others, right?" Rob asked, from the stairs. "Some of us don't have to follow the rules—or the laws."

"Exactly," Gabriel said, with a rather chilling smile. He was walking around the hallway, glancing into each bedroom. "Well, Joyce told us to pick our rooms. I think I'll take . . . this one."

"Hey!" Lewis squawked. "That's the biggest room —the one with the cable hookup and the Jacuzzi and . . . and *everything.*"

Gabriel said blandly, "Thanks for telling me."

"It's much bigger than any of the others," Anna said with quiet heat. "We decided it should go to whoever rooms together."

"You can't just grab it for yourself," Lewis finished. "We ought to *vote.*"

Gabriel's gray eyes narrowed and his lip lifted in something like a snarl. With one step he was close to Lewis. "You know what a lockup cell looks like?" he said, his voice cold and brutal. "It has a two-foot-wide bed and a metal toilet. One metal stool attached to the wall and one built-in desk. That's all. I've been in a cell like that on and off for two years. So now I figure I'm entitled. Are *you* going to do something about it?"

Lewis scratched his nose, looking as if he were considering it. Anna pulled him back a step.

"MTV isn't worth it," she told him.

Gabriel looked at Rob. "You, country boy?"

"I won't fight you, if that's what you mean," Rob drawled. He looked half-disgusted, half-pitying. "Go ahead, take the room—you sad bastard."

Lewis made a faint sound of protest. Gabriel stepped inside his newly acquired room and began to shut the door.

"By the way," he said, turning, "everyone else had better keep out of here. After you spend so much time in lockup, you get to like your space. You get kind of territorial. I wouldn't want anybody to get hurt."

As the door closed, Kait said, "Gabriel—like the angel?" She could hear the heavy sarcasm in her own voice.

The door opened again, and Gabriel gave her a long, measuring look. Then he flashed a brilliant, unsettling smile. *"You* can come in any time you like," he said.

This time after the door slammed, it stayed shut.

*"Well,"* Kaitlyn said.

*"Jeez,"* Lewis said.

Anna was shaking her head. "Gabriel Wolfe—he's not like a wolf, really, because they're very social. Except for a lone wolf, an exile. One that's been driven out of the pack. If wolves get driven out far enough they go a little crazy—start attacking anything that comes near them."

"I wonder what his talent is," Kaitlyn mused. She looked at Rob.

He shook his head. "I don't really know. I met him back in North Carolina—at a place in Durham, another psychic research center."

"Another one?" Lewis said, looking surprised.

"Yeah. My parents took me to see if they could

make any sense of the weird stuff I was doing. I guess his parents did the same thing. He wasn't interested in working with the staff, though. He just wanted his own way, and the hell with other people. A girl ended up . . . getting hurt."

Kait looked at him. She wanted to ask, "Hurt *how?*" but from the closed-off expression on his face, she didn't think she'd get an answer.

"Anyway, that was over three years ago," Rob said. "He ran away from the center right after it happened, and I heard he just went from state to state, getting in a heap of trouble everywhere. *Making* a heap of trouble everywhere."

"Oh, terrific," Lewis said. "And we've got to live with this guy for a *year?*"

Anna was looking at Rob closely. "What about you? Did that center help you?"

"Sure did. They helped me figure out just what it was I was doing."

"And just what *is* it you do?" Kaitlyn put in, staring significantly from him to her leg.

"Healing, I guess," the blond boy said simply. "Some places call it therapeutic touch, some places call it channeling energy. I try to use it to help."

Looking into his steady golden eyes, Kaitlyn felt oddly ashamed. "I'm sure you do," she said, which was as close as she could come to saying "thank you." Somehow she didn't want the others to know what had happened between her and Rob earlier. She felt strangely confused by him—and by her reaction to him.

"I'm sure we all do," Rob said, again simply. His smile was slow but infectious—irresistible, in fact.

"Well, we *try*," Anna said. Kait glanced at Lewis, who just widened his eyes without saying anything. She had the feeling that, like her, he hadn't worked too hard at helping people with his powers.

"Look," Lewis said, clearing his throat. "I don't want to change the subject, but . . . can I pick my room next? Because I'd like . . . ummmm, that one."

Rob glanced into the room Lewis had indicated, then stepped down the hall and looked into two other doors. He turned and gave Lewis an oh-come-on look.

Lewis wilted. "But this is the only one left with cable. And I *need* my MTV. And my computer and my stereo and—"

"There's only one fair thing to do," Rob said. "We should make that room a communal place. That way, everybody can watch TV—there isn't one downstairs."

"But then what do *we* do?" Lewis demanded.

"We double up in the small rooms," Rob said briefly.

Kaitlyn and Anna glanced at each other and smiled. Kaitlyn didn't mind rooming with Anna—she was actually glad. It would be almost like having a sister.

Lewis groaned. "But what about my stereo and stuff? They won't even fit in one of those small rooms, especially if there's two beds in there."

"Good," Rob said relentlessly. "Put 'em in the common room. We can all listen to them. Come on, we'd better start moving furniture."

The first thing Gabriel did was scan the room, prowling around it with silent, wary steps.

He looked in every corner, including the bathroom and closet. It was big, and luxurious, and the balcony offered a quick escape route—if it turned out that escape was necessary.

He liked it.

He flopped on the king-size bed and considered whether he liked anything else about this place.

There was the girl, of course. The one with the witch eyes and the hair like flame. She might be an interesting diversion.

But something inside him twisted uncomfortably. He found himself on his feet and pacing again.

He'd have to make sure it was *just* a diversion. That kind of girl might be too interesting, might tempt you to get involved. . . .

And that could never happen again.

Never. Because . . .

Gabriel wrenched his thoughts away. Aside from the girl, there wasn't much to like here—and several things to hate. Kessler. The restrictions on his freedom—being under house arrest. Kessler. The stupidity of the whole study these people had planned. Kessler.

He could do something about Kessler if he wanted. Take care of him permanently. But then he'd have to run, and if he got caught, he'd end up in lockup until he was twenty-five. It wasn't worth it—not yet.

He'd see how annoying Kessler turned out to be. This place was tolerable, and if he could last out the year, he'd be rich. With that much money, he could *buy* freedom—could buy anything he wanted. He'd wait and see.

And as for them testing his powers—he'd see about that, too. Whatever happened, it was their problem. Their fault.

He settled down on the bed. It was early, but he was tired. In a few minutes he was asleep.

Kait and the others didn't get much moved before Joyce called them down for dinner. Kait rather liked the feeling of eating at the big dining room table with five other people—five, because Gabriel hadn't come out of his room, ignoring all knocks at his door. It was like being part of a large family, and everyone seemed to have a good time—except maybe Marisol, who didn't talk much.

After dinner they went back to furniture arranging. There was plenty of furniture to pick from; the jumble in the hall and rooms seemed to include every style ever invented. Kait and Anna's room ended up with two mismatched single beds, a cheap pressed-wood bookcase, a beautiful French Provincial chair, a Victorian rolltop desk, and the nightstand that had attacked Kait in the hall. Kaitlyn liked all of it.

The bathroom in between the two small rooms was designated the girls' bathroom—by Rob's decree. "Girls need to be nearer to their stuff," he said obscurely to Lewis, who by then only shrugged. The boys would use the bathroom off the common room.

Going to bed, Kaitlyn was happy. Indirect moonlight came in the window behind her bed—*north* light, she noted with pleasure. It shone on the beautiful cedar-and-cherry-bark basket Anna had placed in their bookcase, and on the Raven mask Anna had hung on the wall. Anna herself was breathing peacefully in the other bed.

Kaitlyn's old life in Ohio seemed worlds away—and she was glad.

Tomorrow's Sunday, she thought. Joyce promised to show us the lab, and after that, maybe I'll do some drawing. And then maybe we can look around town. And on Monday we'll go to school and I'll have a built-in set of friends.

What a *wonderful* idea. She knew that Anna and Lewis, at least, would want to eat lunch together. She hoped Rob would, too. As for Gabriel—well, the farther off *he* was, the better. She didn't feel sorry for him at all. . . .

Her thoughts drifted off. The vague discomfort she'd felt about Mr. Zetes had entirely disappeared. She slipped easily into sleep.

And then, suddenly, she was wide-awake. A figure was standing over her bed.

Kaitlyn couldn't breathe. Her heart seemed to fill her mouth and throat, pounding. The moonlight was gone and she couldn't make out any details of the figure—it was just a black silhouette.

For a wild instant—without knowing why—she thought, *Rob? Gabriel?*

Then a dim light came through the window again. She saw the halo of mahogany hair and the full lips of Marisol.

"What's wrong?" she whispered, sitting up. "What are you *doing* here?"

Marisol's eyes were like black pits. "Watch out—or get out," she hissed.

*"What?"*

"Watch out . . . or get out. You kids think you're so smart—so *psychic*—don't you? So superior to everyone else."

Kaitlyn couldn't speak.

"But you don't know anything. This place is different than you think. I've seen things . . ." She shook her head and laughed roughly. "Never mind. You'd just better watch out—" She broke off suddenly and looked behind her. Kaitlyn could see only the black rectangle of the doorway—but she thought she heard a faint rattling sound down the hall.

"Marisol, what—"

"Shut up. I've got to go."

"But—"

Marisol was already leaving. An instant later, the door to Kaitlyn's room silently closed.

**5**

By the next morning, Kait had forgotten about the strange visit.

She woke up to a distant clanging, feeling as if it were very late. A glance at her bedside clock showed that it was seven-thirty, which, of course, meant it was ten-thirty in Ohio.

The clanging was still going on. Anna sat up in bed.

"Good morning," she said, smiling.

"Good morning," Kaitlyn said, feeling how wonderful it was to have a roommate to wake up with. "What's that noise?"

Anna cocked her head. "I have no idea."

"I'm going to find out." Kaitlyn got up and opened the bathroom door. She could hear the clanging more clearly now, and along with it, a weird shouting voice—and a sound like *mooing*.

Impulsively she knocked on the door that led from the bathroom into Rob and Lewis's room. When she heard Rob's voice calling, "Yeah, come in," she opened the door and peered around it.

Rob was sitting up in bed, his rebellious blond hair tousled into a lion's mane. His chest was bare, Kaitlyn noticed with an unreasonable feeling of shock. In the other bed there was a lump of blankets which presumably contained Lewis.

Kaitlyn suddenly realized she was wearing a T-shirt nightgown that only came down to her knees. It had seemed quite natural to walk around in it—until she was confronted by the indisputable reality of *boys*.

She looked desperately around for the source of the clanging and mooing as a distraction. Then she saw it.

It was a cow. A cow made of white porcelain, with a clock in its stomach. The measured, hoarse voice coming from it was shouting in a marked Japanese accent, "Wake . . . *up!* Don't sleep your life away! Wake . . . *up!"*

Kaitlyn looked at the talking alarm clock, and then she looked at Rob. Rob smiled his slow, infectious smile—and suddenly everything was all right.

"It *has* to be Lewis's," Kait gasped, and began to giggle.

"It's great, isn't it?" said a muffled voice from under the blankets. "I got it at Sharper Image."

"So *this* is what I can expect from my housemates," Kait said. "Mooing in the morning." She and Rob were both laughing together now, and she decided it was time to shut the door.

After she closed it, she looked at herself in the bathroom mirror. She didn't usually spend much time at mirrors, but just now . . .

Her hair was rather disheveled, falling in fine tangles to her waist. Wispy red curls had formed on her forehead. Her strangely ringed eyes looked back at her sarcastically.

So you don't care about boys, huh? they seemed to ask. So how come you're thinking that next time you ought to brush your hair before barging in on them?

Kaitlyn turned abruptly toward the shower—and that was when she remembered Marisol's visit.

*"Watch out or get out. . . . This place is different than you think. . . ."*

God, had that really *happened?* It seemed more like a dream than anything else. Kaitlyn stood frozen in the middle of the bathroom, her happiness in the morning draining away. Was Marisol crazy? She must be—she must have some kind of mental trouble, creeping around in the middle of the night and standing over people in bed.

I've got to talk to someone about it, Kait realized. But she didn't know who. If she told Joyce, Marisol might get in trouble. It would be like snitching—and then again, what if it *had* all been a dream?

In the sunlit, bustling morning, with sounds of laughing and washing all around, it was impossible to even consider the idea that Marisol's warning had been genuine. That there really was something wrong at the Institute.

Marisol herself was in the kitchen when Kait went down for breakfast, but she returned Kaitlyn's questioning look with one of sullen blankness. And when Kait said politely, "Marisol, could I talk to you?" she just frowned without looking up from the orange juice she was pouring.

"I'm busy."

"But it's—it's about last night."

She was more than half expecting Marisol to say, "What are you talking about?"—which would mean that it *had* all been a dream. But instead Marisol shook back her mahogany hair and said, "Oh, *that*. Didn't you get it? That was a joke."

*"A joke?"*

"Of course, stupid," Marisol said roughly. "Didn't you know that? You superpsychics are all so stuck-up—couldn't you tell?"

Kaitlyn's temper hit flashover.

"Well, at least we don't sneak around at night acting like lunatics!" she snapped. "The next time you do that, *you'd* better watch out."

Marisol smirked. "Or what?"

"Or . . . you'll see!" Just then the others began arriving for breakfast, so Kaitlyn was spared having to think up a more specific threat. She muttered, "Nut," and snagged a muffin.

Breakfast was lively, just as dinner had been the night before—and just like the night before, Gabriel didn't show up. Kaitlyn forgot all about Marisol as Joyce told them the house rules and described some of the experiments the kids would be doing.

"We'll do one session of testing this morning, just to get some baselines," Joyce said. "But first, anybody who wants to call their parents can do it now. Kaitlyn, I don't think you called your dad yesterday."

"No, but this would be a great time. Thanks," Kait said. She was actually rather glad to get away from the table—looking at Rob's hair in the morning sunlight made her feel strange. She called her father from a phone at the foot of the stairs.

"Are you having a good time, hon?"

"Oh, yes," Kaitlyn said. "It's *warm* here, Dad; I can go out without a sweater. And everybody's nice— almost everybody. Most people. Anyway, I think it's going to be great here."

"And you've got enough money?"

"Oh, *yes.*" Kaitlyn knew her father had scraped together everything he could for her before she left. "I'm going to be fine, Dad. Honest."

"That's terrific, honey. I miss you."

Kaitlyn blinked. "I miss you, too. I'd better go now—I love you." She could hear voices in the room just in front of her. She went around behind the staircase and saw an open door in the little hallway below the landing. Joyce and the others were in a room beyond.

"Come on in," Joyce said. "This is the front lab, the one that used to be a family room. I'm just giving the grand tour."

The lab wasn't at all what Kait had expected. She'd envisioned white walls, gleaming machines, tile floor, a hushed atmosphere. There *were* machines, but there was also an attractive folding screen, lots of comfortable chairs and couches, two bookcases, and a stereo playing New Age music.

"They proved a long time ago at Princeton that a homey atmosphere is best," Joyce said. "It's like the observer effect, you know—psi abilities tend to fade any time the subject is uncomfortable."

The back lab, which had been a garage, was much the same, except that it also had a steel room rather like a bank vault.

"That's for complete isolation in testing," Joyce

said. "It's soundproof, and the only communication with the inside is by intercom. It's also like a Faraday cage—it blocks out any radio waves or other electronic transmissions. If you put someone in there, you can be *sure* they're not using any of their normal senses to get information."

"I bet," Kaitlyn murmured. She could feel a creeping sensation along her spine—somehow she didn't *like* that steel room. "I . . . You're not going to put me in there, are you?"

Joyce glanced at her and laughed, her eyes sparkling like green-blue jewels in her tanned face. "No, we won't put you in there until you're ready," she said. "In fact, Marisol," she added to the college girl behind Kaitlyn, "why don't you go bring Gabriel down here—I think we'll test him in the isolation room for starters."

Marisol left.

"Right, everybody, show time," Joyce said. "This is our first day of experiments, so we'll keep them a bit informal, but I do want everyone to concentrate. I won't ask you to work all the time, but when you *do* work, I ask that you give it your all."

She directed them into the front lab, where she installed Anna and Lewis at what looked like study carrels on either side of the room—study carrels with mysterious-looking equipment. Kaitlyn didn't hear all the instructions she gave them, but in a few minutes both Anna and Lewis seemed to be working, oblivious to anything else in the room.

"Gabriel says he's coming," Marisol announced from the door. "And the volunteers are here. I could only get two so early on Sunday morning."

The volunteers turned out to be Fawn, an extremely pretty blond girl in a motorized wheelchair, and Sid, a guy with a blue Mohawk and a ring in his nose. Very California, Kait thought approvingly. Marisol took him into the back lab.

Joyce gestured at Kait to sit down on a couch over by the window. "You'll be working with Fawn, but you'll have to share her with Rob," she said. "And I think we'll let him go first. So just relax."

Kaitlyn didn't mind—she was both excited and nervous about her own testing. What if she couldn't perform? She'd never been able to use her power on cue—except at Joyce's "vision screening," and then she hadn't *known* she was using her power.

"Now, Rob," Joyce said. She had attached a blood pressure gauge to one of Fawn's fingers. "We'll have six trials of five minutes each. What I'm going to ask you to do is to pull a slip of paper out of this box. If the slip says 'Raise,' I want you to try to raise Fawn's blood pressure. If it says 'Lower,' I want you to try to lower it. If it says 'No change,' I want you to do nothing. Understand?"

Rob looked from Fawn to Joyce, his brow wrinkled. "Yes, ma'am, but—"

"Call me Joyce, Rob. I'll be charting the results. In each case, don't tell anyone what the slip says, just do it." Joyce checked her watch, then nodded at the box. "Go ahead, pick."

Rob started to reach in the box, but then he dropped his hand. He knelt in front of the blond girl's wheelchair.

"Your legs give you much trouble?"

Fawn looked at Joyce quickly, then back at Rob. "I

have MS—multiple sclerosis. I got it early. Sometimes I can walk, but it's pretty bad right now."

"Rob . . ." Joyce said.

Rob didn't seem to hear her. "Can you lift this foot here?"

"Not very high." The leg lifted slightly, fell.

*"Rob,"* Joyce said. "Nobody expects you to . . . We can't *measure* this kind of thing."

"Excuse me, ma'am," Rob said softly, without looking around. To Fawn: "How about this one? Can you lift it some?"

"Not as high as the other." The foot lifted and fell.

"That's just fine. Okay, now, you just hold still. You may feel some heat or some cold, but don't you worry about that." Rob reached forward to clasp the girl's bare ankle.

Joyce tilted her sleek blond head to look at the ceiling, then sighed and went to sit beside Kaitlyn.

"I suppose I should have known," she said, letting her hands with the watch and notebook fall on either side of her.

Kaitlyn was watching Rob.

His head was turned toward her, but he clearly wasn't seeing her. He seemed to be *listening* for something as his fingers moved nimbly over Fawn's ankle. As if looking at the ankle would only distract him.

Kaitlyn was fascinated by his face. Whatever she thought of boys in general, her artist's eye couldn't prevaricate. Words from a book she'd once read ran through her mind: "A beautiful, honest face with the eyes of a dreamer." And the stubborn jaw of a fighter, she added to herself, with an amused sideways glance at Joyce.

"How does that feel?" Rob asked Fawn.

"I . . . sort of tingly," she said, with a breathless, nervous laugh. "Oh!"

"Try to lift this foot again."

Fawn's sneaker came up—almost ten inches off the footrest.

"I did that!" she gasped. "No—*you* did that." She was staring at him with huge eyes full of wonder.

"You did it," Rob said, and smiled. He was breathing quickly. "Now we'll work on the other one."

Kaitlyn felt a stab of jealousy.

She'd never felt anything quite like it before—it was similar to the ache she'd gotten back in Ohio when she'd heard Marcy Huang planning parties. Just now, the way Rob was concentrating on Fawn—and the way Fawn was looking at Rob . . .

Joyce chuckled. "Same thing I saw at his school," she said to Kait in a low voice. "Every girl swooning when he goes by—and him not even knowing what's going on. That boy has no idea he's so sexy."

*That's it,* Kait realized. *He has no clue.* "But *why* doesn't he?" she blurted.

"Probably because of the same thing that gave him his talent," Joyce said. "The accident."

"What accident?"

"He didn't mention it? I'm sure he'll tell you all about it if you ask. He was hang gliding and he crashed. Broke most of his bones and ended up in a coma."

"Oh, my God," Kaitlyn said softly.

"They didn't expect him to live, but he did. When he woke up, he had his powers—but he also had some deficits. Like not knowing what girls are for."

Kaitlyn stared at her. "You're kidding."

"Nope." Joyce grinned. "He's pretty innocent about the world—in a lot of ways. He just doesn't see things quite the way other people do."

Kaitlyn shut her eyes. Of course, that explained why Rob casually reached up girls' skirts. It explained everything—except why just looking at him made her heart pound. And why just the thought of him lying in a coma hurt her. And why she had a very uncharitable desire to run over and physically drag him away from pretty Fawn right now.

There's a word for your condition, her mind told her snidely. It's called—

*Shut up,* Kaitlyn thought. But it was no use. She knew.

"That's enough for now," Rob was saying to Fawn. He sat back on his heels and wiped his forehead. "If we kept working on it every week, I think I could maybe help more. Do you want to do that?"

All Fawn said was, "Yes." But it was the *way* she said it, and the melty, awed way she looked into Rob's eyes, Kait thought. Fortunately, at that moment Joyce stood up.

"Rob, you might talk to *me* about arranging that," she said.

He turned and looked at her mildly. "I knew you'd want me to," he said.

Joyce muttered something under her breath. Then she said, "Right, we'll work something out. Why don't you take a break now, Rob? And, Fawn, if you're too tired for another experiment . . ."

"No, I feel *great,*" Fawn said, not sappily but buoyantly. "I feel so strong—ready for anything."

"Energy transfer," Joyce murmured, taking off the blood pressure cuff. "We'll have to explore that." Then she looked up as the door connecting the front and back labs opened. "What is it, Marisol?"

"He is *not* cooperating," Marisol said. Gabriel was right behind her. He looked particularly gorgeous and somehow elegant—but his expression was one of cold contempt.

"Why not?" Joyce asked.

"You know why," Gabriel said. He seemed to sense Kait's eyes on him, and he gave her a long, deadly look.

Joyce put a hand to her forehead. "Right, let's go talk about it."

Rob reached out and caught her arm. "Ma'am— Joyce—I don't know if that's such a good idea. You want to be careful—"

"I'll handle this, Rob, please," Joyce said, in a voice that indicated she'd had enough. She went into the back lab, taking Marisol and Gabriel with her. The door shut.

Anna and Lewis were looking up from their study carrels. Even Fawn was staring.

Kaitlyn braced herself to look at Rob this close. "What'd you mean by that?" she said, her voice as casual as she could make it.

His gaze seemed to be turned inward. "I don't know—but I remember what happened at that center in Durham. *They* tried to make him do experiments, too." He shook his head. "I'll see y'all later," he said softly, and left. Kaitlyn was pleased that he didn't turn to look back at Fawn, and displeased that he didn't turn to look back at *her*.

A few minutes later Joyce returned, looking slightly frazzled. "Now, where were we? Kaitlyn, it's your turn."

Oh, not now, Kaitlyn thought. She felt raw and throbbing from her new discoveries about Rob—as if she'd had a layer of skin stripped off. She wanted to go off by herself somewhere and think.

Joyce was thumbing through a folder distractedly. "Informal; we'll keep this informal," she murmured. "Kaitlyn, I want you to sit down here." She guided Kaitlyn behind the folding screen, where there was a plush reclining chair. "In a minute I'm going to have you put on these headphones and this blindfold." It was a weird-looking blindfold, like goggles made of the two halves of a tennis ball.

"What's *that?*"

"Poor man's version of a Ganzfeld cocoon. I'm trying to get the money to set up a proper Ganzfeld room, with red lights and stereo sound and all. . . ."

"Red lights?"

"They help induce relaxation—but never mind. The point of Ganzfeld testing is to cut off your ordinary senses, so you can concentrate on the psychic ones. You can't see anything with the blindfold; you can't hear anything because the headphones fill your ears with white noise. It's supposed to help you be receptive to any images that come into your head."

"But images *don't* come into my head," Kait said. "They come into my hand."

"That's fine," Joyce said, and smiled. "Let them come—here's a pencil and paper on a clipboard. You don't need to see to draw; just let the pencil move as it wants to."

It sounded crazy to Kaitlyn, but Joyce was the expert. She sat down and put on the blindfold. Everything went dark.

"We'll try just one target image," Joyce said. "Fawn will be concentrating on a photograph of a certain object. You try and receive her thought."

"Sure," Kaitlyn muttered, and put on the headphones. A sound like a waterfall filled her ears. Must be white noise, she thought, leaning back in the chair.

She felt Joyce put the pencil in her hand and the clipboard in her lap.

Okay, relax.

It was actually rather easy. She knew no one could see her behind the screen—which was a good thing, because she must look pretty silly. She could just stretch out and let her thoughts drift. The darkness and the waterfall noise were like a slippery chute— there was nothing to hold on to. She felt herself sliding down . . . somewhere.

And she began to be afraid. The fear swept up and engulfed her before she knew what was happening. Her fingers clenched on the pencil.

Easy—calm down. Nothing to be scared of . . .

But she *was* scared. There was a terrible sinking in her stomach and she felt as if she were smothering.

Just let images come—but what if there were horrible images out there? Frightening things in the dark, just waiting to get into her mind . . . ?

Her hand began to cramp and itch.

Joyce had said to let the pencil move as it wanted to. But Kaitlyn didn't know if *she* wanted it to move.

Didn't matter. She had to draw. The pencil was moving.

Oh, God, and I have no idea what's coming out, she thought.

No idea—except that whatever it was, was scary. Formless darkness writhed in Kaitlyn's mind as she tried to picture whatever it was that the pencil was drawing.

*I have to see it.*

The tension in her muscles had become unbearable. With her left hand, Kaitlyn pulled the goggles and headphones off.

Her right hand was still moving, like a disembodied hand from a science fiction movie, without her mind having any idea of where it was going to go next. It didn't seem part of her. It was horrible.

And the drawing—the drawing was even more horrible. It was . . . grotesque.

The lines were a little wobbly, but the picture perfectly recognizable. It was her own face. Her face—with an extra eye in the forehead.

The eye had dark lashes all around, so it looked almost insectlike. It was wide and staring and unbelievably repulsive. Kaitlyn's left hand flew to her own forehead as if to make sure there was nothing there.

Only skin puckered with worry. She rubbed hard.

So much for remote vision. She'd bet anything Fawn wasn't out there concentrating on a picture like *this*.

Kaitlyn was about to sit up and tell Joyce that she'd ruined the experiment when the screaming began.

# 6

It was very loud even though it seemed to be coming from far away. The rhythm sounded almost like a baby's crying—the frantic, desperate howls of an abandoned infant—but the voice was much deeper.

Kait dropped the clipboard and vaulted out of the chair. She darted around the folding screen.

Joyce was opening the door to the back lab. Everyone else was staring, apparently frozen. Kait dashed up behind Joyce—just as the screaming stopped.

"Calm down! Just calm down!" Marisol was saying. She was standing in front of the blue-Mohawk guy, who was cringing against the wall. His eyes were wild, his mouth loose and wet with saliva. He seemed to be crying now.

"How long?" Joyce said to Marisol, approaching the Mohawk guy with hands outstretched in an I-mean-no-harm gesture.

Marisol turned. "About forty-five seconds."

"Oh, my God," Joyce said.

"What happened?" Kaitlyn burst out. She couldn't stand to watch this college-age guy cry anymore. "What is going *on* here? What's wrong with him?"

"Kaitlyn, please," Joyce said in a harassed voice.

Kaitlyn looked around the room—and saw that the door to the steel room was opening. Gabriel stepped out with a sneer on his arrogant, handsome face.

"I warned you," he said coldly to Joyce's back.

"This volunteer is a psychic," Joyce said in a thin voice.

"Not psychic enough, obviously," Gabriel said.

"You don't care at all, do you?" a voice said from behind Kaitlyn. She felt herself start—she hadn't heard Rob walk up.

"Rob—" Joyce said, but just then the Mohawk guy made a movement as if to dash away, and she broke off, fully occupied in restraining him.

"I said, you really don't care," Rob was saying, stalking up to face Gabriel. To Kait he looked like a golden avenging angel—but she was worried about him. In contrast to Rob's light, Gabriel looked like dangerous darkness. For one thing, Gabriel had been in jail; if it came to a fight, Kaitlyn would bet he'd fight dirty. And for another, he'd obviously done *something* to that volunteer. He might do it to Rob.

"I didn't arrange this experiment," Gabriel was saying in a frightening voice.

"No, but you didn't stop it, either," Rob snapped.

"I warned them."

"You could have just said no."

"Why should I? I told them what might happen. After that, it's their problem."

"Well, now it's my problem, too."

They were snarling right in one another's faces. The air was thick and electric-feeling with tension. And Kaitlyn couldn't stand it any longer.

"Both of you—*just stop it,*" she exploded, reaching them with three long steps. "Yelling at each other doesn't help anything."

They went on glaring at each other.

*"Rob,"* Kaitlyn said. Her heart was pounding. He looked so handsome, blazing with anger like this— and she could sense he was in danger.

Strangely, it wasn't Rob who responded to her. Gabriel turned his dark, cold gaze away from Rob's face to look at Kaitlyn. He gave her one of his disturbing smiles.

"Don't worry," he said. "I'm not going to kill him—yet. It would violate my parole."

Kaitlyn felt a chill as his gray eyes looked her up and down. She turned to Rob again.

"Please?"

"Okay," Rob said slowly. He took a long breath and she could feel the tension go out of his body. He stepped back.

Everyone seemed to feel the change in atmosphere and relax. Kaitlyn had almost forgotten about the volunteer in the last few minutes, but now she saw that Joyce and Marisol had coaxed him into a chair. He sat with his head bent nearly to his knees.

"Oh, man, what did you do to me?" he was muttering.

"What *did* you do to him?" Rob said to Gabriel. Kaitlyn wanted to know, too—she was *wild* to know —but she was afraid of another flare-up.

Instead, Gabriel just looked grim—almost bitter. "Maybe you'll find out someday," he said significantly, making it a threat.

It was then that Kaitlyn heard Lewis's hesitant voice calling from the front lab.

"Uh . . . Joyce, Mr. Zetes is here."

"Oh, God," Joyce said, straightening up.

Kaitlyn didn't blame her. All the experiments disrupted, everybody standing around, one volunteer practically writhing on the ground . . . It was a lot like getting a visit from the school principal when the class is in a total uproar.

Mr. Zetes was wearing a black coat again, and the two dogs were behind him.

"Problems?" he said to Joyce, who was quickly smoothing down her short blond hair.

"Just a slight one. Gabriel had some difficulties—"

"It looks as if that young man had some, too," Mr. Zetes said dryly. He walked over to the Mohawk guy, looked down at him, then up at Joyce.

"I was going to call an ambulance," she said. "Marisol, would you—"

"There's no need," Mr. Zetes interrupted. "I'll take him in the car." He turned to look at Gabriel, Rob, and Kait, who were all standing by the steel room. "The rest of you young people can take a break," he said.

"Yes, go on. Testing is finished for today," Joyce said, still flustered. "Marisol, why don't you escort Fawn back home? And . . . make sure she's not upset about anything."

Marisol headed for the front lab without changing

71

her sullen expression. Gabriel went, too, with the smooth, long steps of a wolf. Rob hesitated, looking at the Mohawk guy.

"Can I maybe help—"

"No, *thank you*, Rob. If you want some lunch, there are cold cuts in the fridge," Joyce said, in such a voice that Rob had to leave.

Kaitlyn followed, but she paused in the doorway as if trying to shut the door very quietly. It was sheer curiosity; she wanted to know if Mr. Zetes was going to yell at Joyce.

Instead, he said, "How long?"

"About forty-five seconds."

"Ah." It sounded almost appreciative. Kaitlyn got one glimpse of Mr. Zetes, tapping his cane thoughtfully on the ground, and then she had to shut the door.

Gabriel was already gone. Marisol and Fawn were leaving, Marisol looking sullen and Fawn looking back at Rob. Rob was chewing his lip, staring at the floor. Lewis was looking from one person to another. Anna was petting a white mouse she held in her hand.

"Where'd you get that?" Kaitlyn asked. She felt someone ought to say something.

"He was in my experiment. See? This box has different-numbered holes, and I'm supposed to make him go into one of them. Whichever number the monitor shows."

"There must be a sensor inside the hole to register whether you get it right," Lewis said, coming over.

Anna nodded, but she was looking past him. "Don't worry, Rob," she said. "Joyce and Mr. Zetes will take care of that guy. It'll be all right."

"Yeah, but can Mr. Z take care of *Gabriel?*" Lewis said. "That's the question."

Kaitlyn smiled in spite of herself. "Mr. Z?"

"Sure. 'Mr. Zetes' is too long."

"I just don't think he should be here," Rob said broodingly. "Gabriel. I think he's trouble."

"And *I* think I'm going to go crazy wondering what it is he *does,*" Kaitlyn said. "But I don't think Joyce is going to tell us."

"Gabriel has a right to privacy, if he wants it," Anna said gently, putting the mouse in a wire cage. "*I* think we ought to do something to get our minds off it, since we have the afternoon off. We could go into town—or we could finish setting up the common room upstairs."

As always, just being around Anna calmed Kaitlyn down. Serenity drifted from the Native American girl and filled the room.

"Let's do the room," Kaitlyn said. "We can take lunch up there. I'll make sandwiches."

"I'll help," Rob said, and Kaitlyn's heart gave a startled leap.

What do I say, what do I *say?* she thought in the kitchen. Lewis and Anna had gone upstairs; she and Rob were alone.

At least her hands knew what to do. She was used to fixing meals for her dad, and now she spun the lids off mustard jars and stacked cold cuts efficiently. They were very Californian cold cuts: turkey baloney and chicken slices, low-fat salami, Alpine Lace cheese.

Rob worked just as efficiently—but he seemed abstracted, as if his mind were on other things.

Kaitlyn couldn't stand the silence. Almost at random, she said, "Sometimes I wonder if it's really a good idea to try and develop our powers. I mean, look at Gabriel."

She'd said it because she had a vague notion Rob would agree. But he shook his head vigorously and came out of his brown study.

"No, it *is* good—it's important for the world. What Gabriel needs is to develop some *control*—he's bad off for that. Or maybe he just doesn't want to control himself." Rob shook his head and slapped a piece of sprouted whole wheat bread on a sandwich. "But I think everybody ought to develop their talents. D'you realize most people have ESP?" He looked at Kait earnestly.

She shook her head. "I thought we were special."

"We've got more of it. But just about everybody has some. If everybody could work on it—don't you see? Things might start getting better. And they look pretty bad right now."

"You mean . . . for the world?"

He nodded. "People don't care much about each other. But, you know, when I channel energy I feel people's pain. If everybody could feel that, things would be different. There wouldn't be any murder or torture or stuff—because nobody would want to cause pain to anybody else."

Kaitlyn's heart had picked up. He'd "channeled energy" for her—did that mean he felt close to her?

But all she said, very gently, was, "Not everybody can be a healer."

"Everybody has some talent. Everybody could help in some way. When I get out of college I'd like to do the kind of work Joyce is doing—only try to get *everybody* involved in it. Everybody everywhere."

Kaitlyn was staggered by the vision. "You want to save the world?"

"Sure. I'd do my bit," he said, as if saying, *Sure, I'd do my bit for recycling.*

Dear God, Kait thought. I believe him.

There was something about this boy with the golden dreamer's eyes and the quiet voice that commanded her respect. A person like this, Kait thought, comes along only once in a very long time. A person like this can make a difference.

That was what she *thought*. What she felt was . . . was . . . well . . .

Anyway, there was no fighting against it anymore, she thought as they took the sandwiches upstairs.

All through the afternoon, which was spent moving furniture, arguing, and arranging things, Kait hugged her new knowledge to herself. It was both pleasure and pain, just as it was both a pleasure and painful to be able to watch Rob, to be in his company.

She would never have believed she could fall in love on one day's acquaintance.

But there it was. And every minute she was around Rob, the feeling grew stronger. She had trouble focusing on anything else when Rob was in the room, her heart began to beat hard when he looked at her, his voice made her shiver, and when he said her name . . .

By dinnertime, she was a basket case.

The strange thing was, now that she'd admitted it to herself, she wanted to talk about it. To explain to somebody else how she felt. To share it.

Anna, she thought.

When Anna went into their room to clean up before dinner, Kait followed her. She shut the door, then ducked into the bathroom and turned on the faucet.

Anna was sitting on her bed, brushing her long black hair. "What's that for?" she said, amused.

"Privacy," Kait said grimly. She sat down on her own bed, although she could hardly keep herself sitting still. "Anna—can I talk to you?"

"Of course you can."

Of course she could. Kaitlyn knew that suddenly. "It's so strange—back home I never had any friend I could really talk to. But I *know* I can talk to you. I just don't know how to start," she added explosively, discovering this.

Anna smiled, and Kaitlyn felt more peaceful, less agitated. "It wouldn't have anything to do with Rob, would it?"

"Oh, my God," Kaitlyn said, stiffening. "Is it that obvious? Do you think *he* knows?"

"No . . . but I'm a girl, remember? I notice things boys don't notice."

"Yes, well, that's the problem, isn't it?" Kaitlyn murmured, sitting back. She felt crushed suddenly. "I've got this feeling *he* isn't ever going to notice."

"I heard what Joyce said about him."

Kaitlyn was very glad—she wouldn't have to repeat the story, like gossip. "Then you know it's practically hopeless," she said.

"It's not hopeless. You just have to *get* him to notice you, that's all. He likes you; he just doesn't realize you're a girl."

"You think he likes me?"

"Of course he does. And you're beautiful—any

normal guy wouldn't have any trouble seeing you're
female. With Rob, you're just going to have to do
something extra."

"Like take off my shirt?"

"I was thinking of something less extreme."

"I've *thought* of things," Kaitlyn said. "All afternoon I've been thinking of ways . . . well, like trying
to get him into romantic situations. But I don't know
if it's right. Isn't that like tricking him?"

Anna smiled—a very wise smile, Kait thought.
"See that mask?" she said, nodding to the one on the
wall. "That's Skauk, the Raven. He was my great-
grandfather's guardian spirit—and when the mission-
aries came along and gave my family the name
'White,' he was the one who stuck 'Raven' on, so we
would always know who we were. Friends of Raven
the Trickster."

Kaitlyn stared at the mask, with its long, blunt beak,
in fascination.

"Raven was always doing things for his own good—
but they turned out to be for everybody's good in the
end. Like the time when he stole the sun."

Kaitlyn grinned, sensing a story. "When he what?"

"He stole the sun," Anna said gravely, only her eyes
smiling. "Gray Eagle had the sun, but he hated people
so much that he kept it hidden in his house, and
everybody else lived in darkness. Raven wanted the
sun for his own, but he knew Gray Eagle would never
let him inside. So he turned himself into a snow white
bird and tricked Gray Eagle's daughter into letting
him in."

*"Tch,"* Kaitlyn said. Anna's eyes smiled.

"As soon as she did, Raven grabbed the sun and

flew away—but Gray Eagle flew after him. Raven got so scared that he dropped the sun . . . and it landed in the sky, where it lit up the world for everybody."

"That's nice," Kaitlyn said, pleased.

"There're lots of stories about Raven. But the point is, sometimes a little trickery isn't so bad." Anna flashed Kait a dark-eyed glance. "And especially where boys are concerned, I think."

Kaitlyn stood up, feeling excitement churn inside her. "Then I'll do it! If I can think of something good."

"You can start with cleaning up a little," Anna said, laughing. "Right now he'll only notice you for the dirt on your nose."

Kaitlyn not only washed but changed her clothes and pulled her hair back with a gold barrette—but she didn't see that it made any difference in Rob's attitude at dinner. Dinner was novel mostly because Gabriel put in an appearance.

"He eats," Kaitlyn whispered to Anna under cover of passing the brown rice. "I was beginning to wonder."

After dinner, Gabriel vanished again. Lewis and Rob went into the common room, which they now called the study, although Kaitlyn didn't think there was much chance of anyone studying in it. Not with U2 on the CD player competing with a horror movie on the TV. It didn't seem to bother Anna, who curled up in the alcove with a book, but Kaitlyn wanted to get away.

She needed to be by herself because of Rob—and because school was tomorrow, her new school, her new chance. Her feelings were all mixed up, flying around in confusion and bumping into each other and ricocheting off even faster.

But most important, she needed to draw.

Not the ESP kind of drawing. Just regular drawing, which always helped smooth out her thoughts. She hadn't really drawn for two days.

That reminded her of something. The drawing she'd done in the lab—she'd just left it there, behind the folding screen. She should go pick it up sometime; she certainly didn't want anyone else to see it.

"I'll be back in a little while," she said to the others in the study, and then she stopped to be grateful a moment because everybody said good-bye as she left. That had always been one of her dreams, to say to a roomful of people, "I'm going" and have them all say good-bye.

The drawing wasn't in the lab. As she let herself out the back door, she hoped someone had thrown it away.

She took only her sketchbook and a couple of sticks of charcoal—it was too dark outside to really see colors. But there was enough moonlight to see trees, and the air was deliciously fresh and cold.

This is more like winter, she thought. Everything was silver and shadows. In back of the house a narrow dirt road sloped down to a stand of redwood trees. Kaitlyn followed it.

At the foot of the hill was a little, almost dry streambed, with a low concrete bridge crossing it. The road looked as if it were never used. Kaitlyn stood in the middle of the redwoods, breathing in the night and the tree smell.

What a wonderful place. The trees cut off the lights

of the house, and not even U2 could penetrate this far. She felt quite alone.

She sat on a concrete curb with her sketch pad on her knees.

Although the moonlight was beautiful, the coolest kind of light imaginable, there wasn't really enough of it to draw properly. Oh, well, Kaitlyn thought, Joyce wants me to learn how to draw blind. With loose, fluid motions, she sketched in the shapes of some redwoods across the streambed. It was interesting to get only the shape and no detail.

What a peaceful place. She added a bush.

She was feeling much better already. She added a dark, sinuous line for the stream.

A night like this made you believe in magic. She started to add a few rocks—and then she heard a sound.

A thump. Like, Kaitlyn thought, freezing, someone falling out of a tree.

Or jumping.

Strange, how she knew right away it was human. Not an animal sound, and certainly nothing natural.

Someone was out here with her.

She looked around, moving only her head, keeping her body still. She had good eyes, artist's eyes, and when she'd walked down here she'd noticed the shape of the trees and bushes. She ought to be able to spot anything different.

But she couldn't. She couldn't see anything new, and she couldn't hear anything, either. Whoever was out there wasn't speaking.

That made it not funny. Not a joke. When somebody hides at night and doesn't let you know who they are—when you can *feel* eyes on you, but you don't know whose—that wasn't funny. Kaitlyn's hands felt cold and her throat felt very tight.

Just get up. Leave. *Now,* she thought.

She managed two steps up the hill and saw movement among the trees. It was a person, moving out from the cover of the redwoods.

Kaitlyn's body prepared to fight or flee—but not until she saw who it was. She had to see the face before she could be released from paralysis.

The person came closer, feet crunching on dead leaves. Moonlight shone on his face, on slanting eyes and softly curling brown hair. It was the man who'd grabbed her in the airport.

He was wearing regular clothes now, not the red robe he'd worn before. And he was coming straight at her, very quickly.

**7**

**F**ight, Kait decided. Or rather, her body decided it for her, seeming to feel instinctively that she'd never make it up that hill.

Her sketchbook was spiral-bound with heavy wire, and one end was slightly uncoiled—it had been poking her for weeks. Now she dropped the charcoal sticks and brought the book up, poised for attack.

Aim for the eyes, she thought.

She knew she should be screaming, but her throat was too constricted.

All this passed through her mind in the few seconds it took the stranger to reach her. Kaitlyn hadn't been in a fight since elementary school, but now her body seemed to know what to do. The stranger grabbed for her arm—Kaitlyn jerked it away.

*Now,* she thought, and lashed out with the sketch-book. And it worked—the heavy wire caught him in the cheek, tearing a long bloody scratch.

Fierce triumph surged up in Kait. But the next

instant the stranger had her wrist and was twisting it, trying to make her let go of the sketch pad. It hurt, and the pain freed her voice.

"Let go of me," she gasped. *"Let go!"*

He twisted harder. Blood was running down his cheek, black in the moonlight. Kaitlyn tried to kick, but he turned his body and her kicks glanced off harmlessly. He had both her arms now. He was pushing her down onto the sloping ground of the hill. He was winning.

*Scream,* her mind told her.

Kaitlyn sucked in a deep breath and screamed. But it was cut off almost before it started, by the stranger's hand.

"Shut up!" he said, in a furious whisper.

Kaitlyn stared up at him over his smothering hand, knowing her eyes were wide with fear. He was so strong, and so much heavier than she was—she couldn't move at all.

"You're so reckless—you never *think,"* the stranger hissed. The moon was behind him, so his face was in shadow—but she could feel his anger.

He's going to kill me. And I'll never even know why, a small, clear part of her mind said. The rest of her was engulfed in sheer black terror as his hand stayed over her mouth. It was getting very hard to breathe. . . .

Something reared up behind the stranger.

Kaitlyn's dazed mind couldn't tell at first what it was. Just a shape silhouetted against the moonlit sky. Then she saw it was a human shape, with something shining in its hand.

There was a movement quicker than Kait's eyes

could follow, and the stranger on top of her was jerked backward slightly. The moonlight reflected off a knife blade.

"Let go of her," a clipped, harsh voice said, "or I'll cut your throat."

*Gabriel?* Kaitlyn thought in disbelief. But it was true, and now her panicked senses could interpret the scene in front of her. Gabriel was holding the stranger at knifepoint.

The stranger's hands lifted away from Kaitlyn. She drew in a gasping, wheezing breath.

"Now get up," Gabriel said. "Nice and easy. I'm in a bad mood tonight."

The stranger rose in one slow, coordinated motion, like a dancer. The knife stayed at his throat the whole time.

As soon as his weight was removed, Kaitlyn got her feet under her and took two scrambling steps up the hill. Adrenaline was still flooding over her in painful, useless waves. Her hands were shaking.

I should help Gabriel, she thought. No matter how tough he is, he's a kid, and that stranger's a man. A strong man.

"Want me to go back to the house and tell them?" she gasped, trying to make herself sound hard and competent.

"Why?" Gabriel said briefly. He made some movement and the stranger went spinning, landing on his back on the ground.

"Now get out," he said, looking down at the supine figure. "And don't come back unless you're tired of living. If I see you around again, I'll forget I just did two years for murder."

A shock went through Kait. But she didn't have time to think—Gabriel was speaking again.

"I said, get out. Run. Show me a four-minute mile."

The stranger got up, not nearly as smoothly and gracefully as before. From what Kait could see of his expression, he was both furious and frightened.

"You're *both* so stupid—" he began.

*"Run,"* Gabriel suggested, holding the knife as if ready to throw it.

The stranger turned and went, half running, half angrily stalking.

When the crunch of his footsteps had died, Kaitlyn looked at Gabriel, who was folding up the knife and putting it in his back pocket all in one practiced gesture.

Murder, she thought. He was in jail for murder.

What she said, rather unsteadily, was, "Thank you."

He glanced up at her briefly, and she could swear he was amused, as if he knew the difference between her thoughts and her words. "Who was he? An old boyfriend?" he asked.

"Don't be ridiculous," Kait snapped, and then wished she hadn't. One ought to be more polite to a murderer, especially when one was alone with him in the dark. "I don't know *who* he is," she added. "But he was at the airport when I came yesterday. He must have followed Joyce and me home."

Gabriel looked at her skeptically, then shrugged. "I don't think he'll come back." He started toward the house without turning to see if Kait was following.

Kaitlyn picked up her sketchbook and went after him.

*"What happened?"* Rob said, vaulting to his feet. He and Lewis and Anna were in the study—as was Joyce. Kaitlyn had looked for her on the first floor, then come up here.

Rob was staring from Kaitlyn, who was just realizing that she had bits of dead leaves and grass in her hair, to Gabriel, who was behind her. "What happened?" he repeated, in a more controlled but more frightening voice.

"What does it look like?" Gabriel taunted, at his very nastiest.

Rob started toward him, golden eyes blazing.

*"No,"* Kaitlyn said. "Rob, don't. He didn't hurt me; he saved me."

She felt a surge of dizzy excitement—Rob was angry *for* her, protective. But she couldn't let him fight Gabriel.

*"He* saved you?" Rob said, with open scorn. He was on one side of the doorway, staring at Gabriel as if trying to bore holes in him. Gabriel was on the other side, almost lounging against the wall and looking devastatingly handsome. Kait was caught in between them.

She appealed to Joyce, who was rising from the study couch.

"It was that guy, the guy from the airport," she said. "He was out back." She explained what had happened, watching the alarm grow on Joyce's face.

"Jeez, we'd better call the police," Lewis said when

she was done. He sounded more impressed than scared.

"He's right," Anna said, her dark eyes sober.

"Oh, sure, call them," Gabriel sneered. "I only just got paroled. They love to see people like me with switchblades."

Joyce grimaced. She squeezed her eyes shut and did some stretching exercises with her shoulders.

Kaitlyn's heart sank. Gabriel would be in trouble— he might even get sent back to jail. His part of the experiment would be ruined, and he might never learn to control his powers. All because he'd helped her.

Rob was suddenly looking quite cheerful. "Well, we've *got* to report it."

"Fine. Just give me ten minutes' start," Gabriel said through his teeth.

"Stop it, both of you," Kaitlyn said. Then she sighed. Being in love wasn't easy. She didn't want to make Rob unhappy, but she had no choice.

"I have an idea," she said hesitantly. "We could call the police, but not tell them Gabriel was involved. I'll just say I got away from the guy out there. Then nobody would get in trouble, but the police could do whatever they need to."

Rob's smile faded. Gabriel was still glaring. But Joyce opened her aquamarine eyes and beamed.

"Trust you, Kait," she said. "Now, where's a phone?"

Gabriel didn't stay to hear the call.

He went into his room and shut the door behind him. And then, tired but too restless to even sit down, he began to pace.

Images kept floating through his mind. Kaitlyn lying in the moonlight—with some maniac on top of her. What if he hadn't come along just then?

The maniac had been right about one thing—she *was* reckless. She shouldn't be *allowed* out alone at night. She didn't have the right instincts for danger, she wasn't tough enough to protect herself. . . .

So . . . what? his mind asked. So you're going to protect her?

Gabriel flashed one of his best disturbing smiles at nothing. Hardly.

He was going to keep away from her, was what he was going to do. She was a nuisance—and she was stuck on Kessler. Gabriel could see that, even if Kessler was too stupid.

Keep away from her. Yes. And he'd bet—he smiled again—that after what she'd seen tonight, she'd keep away from him.

Two hours later Kait was lying in bed, trying to calm down enough to go to sleep.

There had been a lot of fuss with the police, who'd gone down into the backyard but had found nothing. They'd promised to have a cruiser patrol the area, and Joyce had told the kids to check the door locks and keep a close lookout for strangers from now on.

"And I don't want you going anywhere alone," she told Kait firmly. "Especially at night." Kait was happy to agree.

But now she couldn't sleep. It had all been too weird, too disturbing. Why would some cult guy from the airport follow her home? *Was* he some cult guy? If not, why had he been wearing the robes? A disguise? A stupid one.

What did he *want?*

And beneath all her other thoughts ran a continuous whispering thread. . . .

Gabriel was a murderer.

The others didn't know. Except Rob—Kaitlyn felt sure Rob knew. But even not knowing, they'd treated him pretty badly tonight. No one had said anything complimentary about him saving Kait. Lewis and Anna had kept their distance, as if they expected him to pull a switchblade on *them* at any minute, and Rob had watched him with steady, smoldering fury.

Rob—she *wouldn't* think about Rob now. She couldn't take the agitation.

Anna was breathing peacefully on the other side of the bedroom. Kaitlyn glanced at her, a motionless shape in the darkness, then very carefully and quietly got out of bed.

She shouldered into her robe and slipped noiselessly out the door.

The study was dim. Kait sat on the window seat in the alcove, her chin on her knees. Outside, a few lights shone through waving tree branches. Then she noticed that light was also shining through the curtains in Gabriel's room.

What she did then was born of sheer impulse. If she'd thought about it, she never would have gone through with it. But she didn't give herself time to think.

She jumped off the window seat and went to knock on his door.

A very quiet knocking, in case he was asleep with the light on. But after only an instant the door opened.

He was wearing a rather sleepy scowl.

"What?" he said ungallantly.

"Come into the study," Kaitlyn whispered.

The scowl disappeared, changing into a dazzling bared-teeth smile. "No, *you* come in *here.*"

He was daring her, Kaitlyn realized. All right; great. She'd prove she trusted him.

Head very high, back straight, she swept by him. She sat down on the desk chair. She glanced around unobtrusively—the room was as nice as Lewis had said. Huge bed, matching furniture, *acres* of space. It seemed bare of personal possessions, though. Maybe Gabriel didn't have any.

Slowly, watching her, Gabriel sat down on the bed. He'd left the door a little ajar. Kaitlyn, motivated by she didn't know what, got up and closed it.

"You're crazy, you know," Gabriel said unemotionally, as she resumed her seat.

"I wanted to say thank you," Kaitlyn said. *And that I'm not afraid of you,* she added silently. She still couldn't figure out what she felt about Gabriel—even whether she liked him or hated him.

But he had saved her from a very bad situation.

Gabriel didn't look gratified by the thanks. "And that's all?" he said mockingly.

"Of course."

"You're not just a little curious?" When Kaitlyn blinked at him, he leaned forward. His teeth were bared again. "You don't even want to know?"

Kaitlyn felt distaste pinching her features. "You mean . . . about . . ."

"The murder," Gabriel said, his dazzling grin getting nastier by the minute.

Fear uncoiled in Kaitlyn's stomach. He was right—

she *was* crazy. What was she doing sitting here in his bedroom? Two days ago she wouldn't have sat in *any* guy's bedroom, and now she was chatting with a killer.

But Joyce wouldn't have brought him to the Institute if he was really dangerous, she thought. Joyce wouldn't take that risk.

Kaitlyn said slowly, "Was it really murder?" Then she looked straight up at Gabriel.

His expression changed as he met her eyes—as if she'd startled him. Then he seemed to regain his balance.

"*I* called it self-defense, but the judge didn't agree," he said. His eyes were now cold as ice.

Something inside Kaitlyn relaxed. "Self-defense," she said.

Gabriel looked at her for a long moment, then away. "Of course, the other one wasn't self-defense. The first one."

He's trying to shock you, Kaitlyn told herself.

He's succeeding, her mind whispered back.

"I'd better go," she said.

He was *very* fast. She was closer to the door, but before she could reach it, he was in front of her, blocking it.

"Oh, no," he said. "Don't you want to hear all about it?"

Those dark gray eyes were strange—almost fixed, as if he were looking through her. His expression was strange, too. As if he were covering unbearable tension with mockery and derision. Kaitlyn could see the glint of clenched teeth between his parted lips.

"Stop it, Gabriel," she said. "I'm going."

"Don't be shy."

"I'm not *shy,* you jerk," she snapped. "I'm just sick of you." She tried to push past him and he wouldn't let her. They tussled.

Kaitlyn found out very quickly how much stronger he was.

Stupid, *stupid,* she thought, trying to get a hand free to hit him. How had she gotten herself *into* this mess? Her heart was going like a trip-hammer, and her chest felt as if it would burst. She was going to have to scream—unless he stopped her. Choked her, maybe. Was that what he'd done to the others?

Maybe he'd used a knife. Maybe he cut them. Or maybe it had been something even worse. . . .

She and Gabriel had been struggling silently, their faces inches apart. Kaitlyn's mind was dark with imaginings of how he might have killed before.

And then . . .

And then it all stopped. Kaitlyn's fantasies were cut off as if somebody had slammed down a window in her mind. And all because of the look in Gabriel's eyes.

Grief. Guilt, too, plenty of that, but mainly grief. A kind Kaitlyn recognized, the kind that makes you nearly bite through your lip so you won't make a noise. The kind Kaitlyn could remember from when she was eight years old, when her mother died.

Gabriel, with his handsome, arrogant face, and his savage bared teeth, was trying to make the tears go away.

Kaitlyn stopped struggling with him, realizing in the moment she did that he hadn't hurt her. He'd been blocking her, restraining her, but he hadn't bruised her.

"Okay," she said, her voice loud in the silence. "So tell me, then."

It caught him off guard. Actually rocked him backward. For a moment he looked shocked—and vulnerable.

Then his face hardened. He was taking it as a challenge.

"I will," he snarled back. He let go of her and stepped away—a hunted, constrained movement. His chest was rising and falling quickly.

"You've all been wondering what I *do,*" he said. "Haven't you?"

"Yes," Kait said. She moved cautiously away from the door. "Is that so surprising?"

"No." He laughed—a very bitter laugh. "It's what everyone wants to know. But when they find out, they don't like it." He turned and looked at her with mock bewilderment. "For some reason, they seem to be scared of me."

Kaitlyn didn't smile. "I know what it's like," she said flatly to the carpet. "When they're scared of you. When they can't look you in the eye and they kind of edge away when you get close . . ." She looked up at him.

Something flickered in his eyes; then he shook his head, turning away. "You don't know what it's like when they're so scared that they *hate* you. When they want to *kill* you because they're so scared that you'll . . ."

"That you'll what?"

"Read their minds. Steal their souls. Take your pick."

There was a silence. Ice crept along Kaitlyn's spine. She was bewildered—and afraid.

"Is that what you do?" she said, fighting to keep her voice above a whisper.

"No." The cold knot in Kaitlyn's stomach loosened slightly—until he turned around and looked at her with the calm gray eyes of a madman. "It's not as simple as that. Do you want to know how it works?"

Kaitlyn didn't move, didn't speak. She just looked at him.

He spoke precisely, as if giving a lecture. "Any time two minds make contact, there's a transfer of energy. That's what contact *is,* the transfer of a certain kind of energy. Back and forth, energy carrying information. You understand?"

Rob had talked about energy—channeling energy. But maybe that had been a different kind.

"Go on," Kaitlyn said.

"The problem is that some minds are stronger than others. More powerful. And if a strong mind contacts a weaker one—things can get out of control." He stopped, looking at the dark, curtained window.

"How?" Kaitlyn whispered. He didn't seem to hear her. "How can it get out of control, Gabriel?"

Still looking at the window, he said, "You know how water flows from a high place to a low place? Or how electricity keeps trying to find a ground for its force? Well, when two minds touch, energy flows. Back and forth. But the stronger mind always has more pull."

"Like a magnet?" Kaitlyn asked quietly. She'd

never been great at science, but she did know that—the bigger the magnet, the stronger it was.

"A magnet? Maybe at first. But if something happens—if things get off balance—it's more like a black hole. All the energy flows out of the weaker mind. The strong one drains it. Sucks it dry."

He was standing very still, every muscle rigid. His hands were shoved in his pockets, fingers clenched. And his gray eyes were so bleak and lonely that Kaitlyn was glad he wasn't looking at her.

She said, evenly, "You're a telepath."

"They called it something different. They called me a psychic vampire."

*And I felt sorry for myself,* Kaitlyn thought. *Just because I couldn't help people, because my drawings were useless. But his gift makes him kill.*

"Does it *have* to be that way?"

He flicked a glance at her, eyes narrowing. He'd heard the pity in her voice.

"Not if I keep the contact short. Or if the other mind is fairly strong."

Kaitlyn was remembering. *How long? About forty-five seconds. Oh, my God.*

And the Mohawk guy had come out screaming.

*This volunteer is a psychic. Not psychic enough, obviously.*

How strong did a mind need to be to hold up to Gabriel?

"Unfortunately," Gabriel said, still watching her with narrowed eyes, "even a little thing can upset the balance. It can happen before you know it."

Kaitlyn was afraid.

A bad thing to be around Gabriel. He saw it, sensed

it. And it obviously triggered some instinct in him—to go for the throat.

He gave one of his wild, disturbing smiles. There was bright sickness in his eyes. "That's why I have to be so careful," he said. "I have to stay in control. Because if I lose control, things can happen."

Kaitlyn struggled to breathe evenly. He was moving closer to her, like a wolf scenting something it wanted. She forced herself not to cower, to look at him without flinching. She put steel into her neck.

"That was how it happened the first time," Gabriel told her. "There was a girl at that center in Durham. We liked each other. And we wanted to be together. But when we got close—something happened."

He was directly in front of her now. Kaitlyn felt her back flatten against the wall.

"I didn't mean it to happen. But I got emotional, you see. And that was dangerous. I wanted to be closer, and the next thing I knew, we were linking minds." He stopped, breathing quickly and lightly, then went on. "She was weak—and afraid. Are you afraid, Kaitlyn?"

# 8

Lie, Kaitlyn thought. But she felt sure he could detect a lie. She also felt sure the truth might kill her.

Nothing to do but take the offensive.

"Do you want me to be? Is that what you want—for it all to happen again?"

A veil-like spiderweb seemed to fall over his gray eyes, taking out their dark brightness. He even pulled back a fraction.

Kaitlyn stayed on the attack. "I don't think you meant to hurt that girl. I think you loved her."

He stepped back even farther.

"What was her name?" Kaitlyn said.

To her surprise, he answered. "Iris. She was just a kid. We were both kids. We had no idea what we were doing."

"And she was there because she was psychic?"

His lip curled. " 'Not psychic enough,' " he quoted, as if giving Kait the answer she was expecting. Stark bitterness was in his eyes. "She didn't have enough

. . . whatever. Life force. Bioenergy. Whatever it is that makes people psychic—and keeps them alive. That night at the center . . . by the time I was able to let go of her, she was just limp. Her face was white, blue-white. She was dead."

His chest heaved, and then he said deliberately, "No life. No energy left. I'd drained her dry."

Kaitlyn wasn't on the offensive any longer, and she couldn't hold his gaze. Her own chest felt as if there were a tight band around it. After a moment she said quietly, "You didn't do it on purpose."

"Didn't I?" he said. He seemed to have conquered whatever emotion had possessed him; he was breathing easily again. When Kait looked up, she saw his gray eyes were no longer bitter, or even shielded. They were . . . empty.

"The people at the center had a different idea," he went on. "When I realized she wasn't breathing, I called for help. And when they came and saw her—all blue like that—they thought the worst. They said I'd attacked her. They said I'd tried to force her, and when I couldn't, I killed her."

Kait felt a wash of pure, dizzying horror. She was glad there was a wall behind her; she let her weight rest on it, and only then realized she'd shut her eyes.

"I'm sorry," she whispered, opening them. Then, trying to find some comfort, she said, "Rob was right. What Joyce is doing *is* important for the world. We all need to learn how to control our powers."

Gabriel's face twisted. "You believe that country-boy stuff?" he said with utter contempt.

Kaitlyn was taken aback. "Why do you hate Rob so much?"

"Didn't you know? The golden boy was there, in Durham. They practically worshiped him—everything he did was right. And *he* was the one who figured out what had happened to Iris. He didn't know how I'd done it, but he knew her energy had been tapped, like blood if you cut an artery. They hunted me, you know. Like an animal. The center and the police and everyone." His voice was dispassionate.

But that wasn't Rob's fault, Kait thought. It *wasn't*. Aloud she said, "So you went on the run."

"Yeah. I was fourteen and stupid. Lucky for me, they were stupider. It took them a year to find me, and by then I was in California. In jail."

"For another murder," Kaitlyn said steadily.

"When the world is so stupid, you take your revenge, you know? People deserve it. Anybody that weak deserves it. The guy I killed tried to mess with me. He wanted to shoot me over the five dollars in my pocket. I got him first."

Revenge, Kaitlyn thought. She could picture the parts of the story Gabriel hadn't told. Him running away, not caring what happened to him, not caring what he did. Hating everything: the universe, for giving him his power; the stupid weak people in the universe, for being so easy to kill; the center, for not teaching him how to control his gift—and himself. Especially himself.

And Rob, the symbol of someone who'd succeeded, whose powers brought only good. Who was in control. Who still *believed* in something.

"He's an idiot," Gabriel said, as if reading her thought. He did that too much; it bothered Kaitlyn. "Him and those other two, they're all idiots. But you have some common sense—or at least I thought you did."

"Thanks," Kait said dryly. "Why?"

"You see things. You know something's wrong here."

Kaitlyn was startled. "Something wrong? You mean, at the Institute?"

He gave her a look of knowing contempt. "I see. That's how you're going to play it."

"I'm not *playing* anything—"

He flashed a disturbing smile and turned, walking to the center of the room. "After all, if you leave, you don't stand much chance of getting him. Can't reel him in from Ohio."

Kaitlyn felt herself flush with anger.

It was over—the confidences, Gabriel's almost-decency, his letting down of walls. He was going to be as nasty and objectionable as possible now, just so she wouldn't get the wrong idea about him. Like that he was an okay person.

Well, I won't rise to it, Kaitlyn thought. I won't even dignify that with an answer. And however it sounds, he can't really *know* what Anna and I talked about behind closed doors.

She pushed herself off the wall and moved one step toward Gabriel. She said, very formally, "I'm sorry for what happened to you. It was all terrible. But I think that you should start thinking about what you can do to change things from now on."

Gabriel smiled silkily from behind his walls. "But what if I don't want to change things?"

Two minutes ago, Kaitlyn had been dizzy with

sympathy for him. Now she wanted to kick him in the shins.

*Boys,* she thought.

"Good night, Gabriel," she said.

You jerk.

He widened his eyes. "Don't you want to stay? It's a big bed."

Kaitlyn didn't bother to answer that at all. She went out with her head very high, muttering words that would have shocked her father.

One thing was fortunate. For a while there, she'd felt quite close to Gabriel—and that could have meant trouble. Imagine her, Kaitlyn the cold, falling for not just one but *two* boys. But he'd taken care of that. He'd pushed her away, and she felt certain he wouldn't let her ever get close again.

No, thank God, she wasn't in any danger. She found Gabriel interesting—even, in a weird way, heart-breaking—and he was certainly gorgeous. But . . . well, anyone with the bad luck to fall in love with *him* would have to disembowel herself with a bamboo letter opener.

She wouldn't tell anyone what he'd told her about his power. That would be betraying a confidence. But she thought she might talk with Rob about him someday. It might change Rob's views, to know that Gabriel could feel regret.

Strangely, when Kait got back to bed, she fell asleep at once.

The next day Joyce took them to San Carlos High School. They were already registered for classes, and

Kait was delighted to find that she shared sociology

Kait was delighted to find that she shared sociology and British literature with Anna and Rob. In fact, she was delighted with everything. She'd never dreamed school could be like this.

It was different from Ohio. The campus itself was bigger, more sprawling, more open in design. Instead of one big building, there were lots of little ones, connected by covered paths. Ridiculous if it snowed —but it *never* snowed here. Never.

The buildings were more modern, too. Less wood, more plastic. Smaller rooms with more crowding. No brick, no peeling paint, no wheezing furnace.

The students seemed friendly—Rob's blond good looks had something to do with that, Kaitlyn thought. He was clearly a high-status, desirable boy, and he ate lunch with her and Anna and Lewis. Kait could see the glances other girls shot at their table.

Anna was clearly high-status, too—because she was beautiful, not at all nervous, and she didn't seem to care if anyone approached her. By the end of lunch, several girls had come by offering to show the newcomers around. They stayed to chat. One mentioned a party on Saturday.

Kait was very happy.

The thing she'd worried most about was explaining why she and the others were living together. She didn't want to tell these California girls anything about psychic powers and the Institute. She didn't want to be different at this school. She wanted to *fit in*.

But fortunately Lewis took care of that. Between snapping pictures of the girls, he grinned and said that a nice old man had given them a lot of money to go to school here. No one believed him, but it created an irresistible aura of mystery that enhanced their status even more.

At the end of the day, Kaitlyn walked out of art studio class feeling blissful. The art teacher had called her portfolio "impressive" and her style "fluid and arresting." All she wanted to make the world perfect was Rob.

Gabriel, of course, didn't associate with anyone, and ate lunch alone. Kaitlyn saw him several times that day, always away from people, always with his lip curled. He could have had tremendous status himself, she thought, because he looked so handsome and moody and dangerous, but he didn't seem to want it.

Marisol collected them after school in a silver-blue Ford van—all except Gabriel, who didn't show up at the pickup point. Kaitlyn thought about his parole and hoped he was on his way back to the Institute.

"Now for some testing," Joyce said when they got home.

That was fine with Kaitlyn. She was jubilant from her first day at school, and an afternoon of testing meant an afternoon with Rob. She still hadn't figured out a plan for helping him discover she was female, but it was always at the back of her mind. Maybe an opportunity would come up spontaneously.

But the first thing Joyce did was send Rob upstairs, saying she'd call him after she got the others settled.

"The REG is ready, Lewis," she added. She sat Lewis down at the same study carrel as before. This time Kait was bold enough to come up behind them.

"What is that thing?" she asked, looking at the

machine in front of Lewis. It looked like a computer, but the monitor had a grid-marked screen with a wiggly green line running across the middle. Like a hospital monitor charting a patient's heartbeat.

"This is a random event generator," Joyce said. "It's a computer that only does one thing—it spits out random numbers. It's producing numbers right now, some positive, some negative, all completely random. That's what the green line is charting. Lewis's job is to make the line go up higher—to influence the machine to spit out more positive numbers than negative ones."

"You can do that?" Kait asked, looking at Lewis in surprise. "With your mind?"

"Yeah, that's what PK is. Mind over matter. This is actually a lot easier than making dice come up a certain number—but I can do that, too, sometimes."

"Stay away from Vegas, kid," Joyce said, rapping him on the head with her knuckles. "They'd shoot out your kneecaps."

She turned to Anna. "Right, you. Same as yesterday. I want you to tell that mouse which hole to go in."

Anna already had the white mouse out of its cage. "Come on, Mickey. Let's go make history."

"Right. Now, Kaitlyn," Joyce said. She nodded Kait toward the folding screen, where Marisol was wheeling up a machine on a cart. Kaitlyn eyed the dials and wires apprehensively.

"Don't be nervous. It's just an EEG machine," Joyce said. "An electroencephalograph. It records your brain waves."

"Oh, great."

"That isn't the part you're not going to like. You're going to really hate *this.*" She held up what looked like a tube of toothpaste. "It's electrode cream, and it's murder to get out of your hair."

Kaitlyn sat in the reclining chair, resigned.

Marisol's thickly lashed brown eyes met Kait's only for the briefest of moments. Her full lips were curved in a bored, unchanging pout.

"This is just prep stuff to clean your skin," she said, squeezing a plastic bottle over a ball of cotton. She swabbed several places on Kaitlyn's head, forehead, and temples.

"Don't move your head." She dabbed some of the toothpaste on Kaitlyn's temple, then dabbed more on an electrode. Kaitlyn watched out of the corner of her eye as the wicked-looking little thing was stuck to her.

It didn't hurt. It tickled slightly. Kait shut her eyes and relaxed until Marisol finished wiring her up.

"Now, Medusa," Joyce said. "As I said, we're going to monitor your brain waves while you're doing your stuff. Brain wave levels change depending on what you're doing: Beta waves show you're attending to something, theta waves show you're drowsy. We're looking for alpha waves—the ones usually associated with psychic activity."

She saw Kaitlyn's expression and added, "Just try to ignore all this equipment, right? You'll be doing exactly the same thing as yesterday."

Kaitlyn looked sideways without moving her head, and saw Marisol bringing two strangers into the lab. New volunteers. Kaitlyn felt a sudden sharp twinge.

"Joyce, is one of those volunteers . . . for Gabriel?"

"I don't know where Gabriel is—although I'd like to," Joyce said grimly, handing Kait a pencil and clipboard. "Now relax, kiddo. No blindfold or earphones this time."

Kaitlyn shut her eyes again. She could hear some activity on the other side of the folding screen—Joyce giving a photo to the volunteer.

"Right," Joyce said. "The subject is concentrating, Kait. You try and receive her thought."

It was only then that Kait discovered how anxious she was. Yesterday she hadn't known what to expect. Today she did know, and she was uneasy. Worried that she wouldn't be able to perform—and worried that she would.

She didn't feel like sliding down that mental chute into nothingness again. And if she did succeed . . . what if she drew something as grotesque as yesterday's picture?

Don't think about it. Take it easy. This is what you're *here* for, remember?

Don't you want to learn to control your power?

Kaitlyn gritted her teeth, then made a supreme effort to relax, to tune the world out. She could hear muted voices.

"Still beta waves on the EEG." That was Marisol.

"Give her time." That was Joyce.

Be calm, Kaitlyn thought. Ignore them. The chair's comfortable. You didn't get much sleep last night.

Slowly, gradually, she felt herself sink into drowsiness.

"Theta waves."

Blackness, falling . . .

"Alpha waves."

"Good!"

Kaitlyn's hand began to cramp and itch. But as she lifted the pencil, eyes shut, she suddenly remembered yesterday's picture. Anxiety twisted in her stomach.

"Back to beta waves," Marisol said, as if announcing a death in the family.

Joyce peered around the screen. "Kaitlyn, what's wrong?"

"I don't know." Now Kait felt guilty as well as anxious. "I just can't focus."

"Hmm." Joyce seemed to hesitate, then she said, "Right, wait a sec," and disappeared.

She was back again quickly. "Shut your eyes, Kait."

Kaitlyn obeyed automatically. She felt a quick dab and then the touch of something cold on her forehead. Very cold.

"Now try again," Joyce said, and Kait heard her go.

Again Kait tried to relax. This time she felt the darkness swirl around her immediately. Then she had an odd sensation, a feeling of pressure in her head. Like an explosion building. And then—

—pictures. Images rushing in, almost with more force than Kaitlyn could stand.

"Alpha waves like crazy," a faraway voice said. Kaitlyn scarcely heard it.

Nothing like this had ever happened to her before—but she was too startled to be afraid. The pictures were kaleidoscopic, each passing in a flash almost before she could recognize it.

Gabriel. Something purple. Joyce—or someone like her. Something purple and irregular. A doorway with someone standing in it. A bunch of purple round things. Something tall and white—a tower? A bunch of purple . . . grapes.

She could feel her hand moving, drawing small circles over and over on the paper. She couldn't help opening her eyes—and the instant she did, the images in her head vanished.

She'd drawn a bunch of grapes. Made sense. That was the picture she'd gotten most frequently.

Recklessly, ignoring the wires, she stood up and looked around the screen.

"What happened?" she demanded of Joyce. "I saw pictures in my head—what did you *do?*"

Joyce stood up quickly. "Just put on another electrode."

Kaitlyn put a hand to her forehead. It felt as if there was something between the electrode and the skin.

"Over your third eye," Marisol added stonily.

Joyce glanced back at her. Marisol's olive-skinned face was expressionless.

Kaitlyn had frozen. Her drawing yesterday . . . "What's—what's a third eye?"

"According to legend, it's the seat of all psychic power," Joyce said lightly. "It's in the center of your forehead, where the pineal gland is."

"But—but why would an electrode—"

"God, she's still in alpha waves," Marisol interrupted.

"Time to get you unwired," Joyce said briskly. She began pulling electrodes off. Kaitlyn felt the forehead one go, but Joyce's hands moved so quickly, she didn't see what became of it.

"By the way, what did you get?" Joyce asked, taking the clipboard from her. "Oh, *terrific,*" she cried. "Oh, look at this, everybody!"

The warmth in her voice made Kaitlyn forget what she'd been upset about.

"I don't believe it—you got the target picture exactly, Kait! *Exactly,* down to the number of grapes on the bunch."

Anna and Lewis were crowding around. The volunteer, a tall girl with night-dark skin, showed Kait the photo she was holding. It was a bunch of grapes—and Kait's own drawing might have been traced directly from it.

"That's impressive," a warm, drawling voice said from behind Kaitlyn. She felt her heart pick up speed.

"I think it was an accident," she told Rob, turning.

"No accident," Joyce said. "Good concentration. And a good volunteer; we'll have to have you back."

Rob was looking at Kaitlyn's face, his golden eyes darkening. "Are you okay? You look kind of tired."

"Actually—this is so strange—I just got a headache." Kait put her fingers to the center of her forehead, where pain like an ice pick had suddenly begun jabbing. "Oh—I guess I didn't get enough sleep last night. . . ."

"I think she needs a break," Rob said.

"Of course," Joyce said at once. "Why don't you go upstairs and lie down, Kait? We're done here."

Kait was wobbly on her feet.

"I'll help," Rob said. "Hold on to me."

It was the perfect opportunity; better than any plan or trick Kaitlyn could have thought up. And it was *useless,* because all at once her head hurt so badly that she only wanted to lie down and go to sleep.

The pain came in throbbing waves. Rob had to lead her into her bedroom because she couldn't see straight.

"Lie down," he said, and turned off the bedside lamp.

Kaitlyn eased down, then felt the mattress give under Rob's weight beside her. She didn't open her eyes. She couldn't; even the diffuse afternoon light from the window hurt.

"It sounds like a migraine," Rob said. "Is the pain all on one side?"

"It's here. In the middle," Kaitlyn whispered, indicating the spot. Now she was feeling waves of nausea. Oh, *wonderful.* How romantic.

"Here?" Rob said, sounding surprised. His fingers on her forehead were blessedly cool. Strange; they'd been warm last time.

"Yes," Kaitlyn whispered wretchedly. "I'll be all right. Just go away." And now, to top everything off, she'd told the boy she loved to get lost.

Rob ignored the suggestion. "Kait, I was wrong. It's not a migraine; it's not even an ordinary headache. I think you're sick from burning energy too fast—psychic energy. You've run yourself dry."

Kaitlyn managed a feeble "So?"

"So—I can help you. If you'll let me."

For some reason, that frightened Kaitlyn. But a stab of agony made up her mind. "All right . . ."

"Good. Now, relax, Kaitlyn." Rob's voice was soft but commanding. "It may feel strange at first, but don't fight it. I have to find an open transfer point. . . ."

Cool, deft fingers touched either side of Kaitlyn's neck, paused for a moment as if searching for something. Then lifted, not finding it. They moved to probe delicately at the tender area behind the jaw. "No . . ." Rob murmured.

Kaitlyn felt her hand gently taken. Rob's thumb centered on her palm, his index finger directly opposite it on the back of her hand. Again he seemed to be searching for something, moving his fingers minutely. Almost like a nurse feeling for a vein before taking blood.

"No."

Rob shifted. "Let's try this—move that way a little." Kaitlyn followed his urging and scooted toward the side of the bed. She opened her eyes automatically—and then quickly shut them in alarm. Rob was bending over her, his face very close. Suddenly a pounding heart added to her pain.

"What . . . ?" she gasped.

"This is just one of the most direct ways to transfer energy," he said simply. "You need a lot."

His lack of embarrassment or self-consciousness saved her. Kaitlyn kept her eyes shut and held still as he put his forehead to hers. Their lips were almost touching.

"Got it," he murmured. His mouth actually brushed hers, but he didn't seem to notice. "Now . . . think about where it hurts. Concentrate on the place."

A minute ago she hadn't been able to think about anything else. But now . . . Kaitlyn's awareness was

111

flooded with *him*. She didn't want to move or breathe. She could sense his entire body, even though only his forehead was touching her. Third eye to third eye, she thought dizzily.

Then, all at once, a new sensation rushed in and drove out all thought of anything physical. It was so new that she didn't have any way to classify it.

It wasn't like sight, or touch, or taste, but Kaitlyn's fogged brain tried to interpret it that way. If it had been sight, it would have been millions of sparkling lights that glowed and glittered like jewels. A dynamic, changing pattern of multicolored sparks, twinkles, and flares.

If it had been touch, it might have been pressure— not an uncomfortable pressure, but one that swept away all the pain of her headache. Like a river rushing through her mind, clearing out everything stagnant and clotted and decayed.

If it had been taste, it would have been like fresh, pure water—water she drank greedily, like an exhausted runner whose mouth has been full of choking dust.

It was electrifying—overwhelming. It didn't simply take away the pain. It filled her with life.

Kaitlyn never knew how long she lay drinking in the life-giving energy. But some time later, she realized that Rob was slowly sitting up. She opened her eyes.

They looked at each other.

"I . . . thank you," Kaitlyn said, barely above a whisper.

She expected him to smile and nod. Instead he blinked. It was the first time she'd seen him at a loss for words.

And then, as they looked at each other, a simple thing happened. Neither of them looked away. With ordinary friends you always look away after a moment —or you speak.

But Rob didn't speak and he didn't look away.

The air between them seemed to shimmer.

# 9

It was as if Rob were seeing her for the first time. More than that—it was as if he were seeing a *girl* for the first time. He looked astonished and wondering, like a person who had never heard music before suddenly catching a few notes of a beautiful melody on the wind. Catching it and wanting desperately to follow it.

His expression was that of someone on the brink of the greatest discovery of his life.

"Kaitlyn?" he whispered, and his voice was awed and questioning and almost frightened.

Kaitlyn couldn't speak. They were both on the threshold of something so big—so *transforming*—that it terrified her. It would change everything, forever. But she *wanted* it. She wanted it to happen.

The whole universe seemed to be hushed and waiting, breath held.

But Rob didn't move. He was on the brink of discovery—but not there yet.

He needs help, Kaitlyn thought. He still doesn't understand what's going on.

It was up to her to show him, to help him take that first step—if she wanted to. And she did. Kaitlyn suddenly felt calm and clear. She saw in her mind what was going to happen, like a picture already finished.

She would cradle his face with her hands and kiss him—very softly. And Rob would look at her with such surprise. So completely innocent—but not stupid. Rob wasn't slow to catch on. After she kissed him the second time, the astonishment would turn to dawning wonder. His golden eyes would start smoldering the way they did when he was angry . . . but for a very different reason.

Then he'd put his arms around her, and kiss her—so lightly—and the energy, the healing energy, would flow between them. And everything would be wonderful.

Breath held, Kaitlyn reached up to touch Rob's face, seeing her own graceful artist's fingers on his jaw. Even that little contact sent sparks dancing up her palm. It all seemed so simple and natural—as if she knew what to do without thinking. As if she'd always known, in some wise place inside.

Imagine it—Kaitlyn the cold, knowing what to do, feeling so sure. It was all about to happen.

Then voices broke into her reverie. Laughing, ordinary voices that didn't belong at all to the beautiful new world Kaitlyn was inhabiting. She looked up in confusion.

Lewis and Anna were just outside the door. Gabriel was behind them.

"Hey, Kait," Lewis began cheerfully. And then, seeing her face, "Uh, oops."

Anna's dark eyes were stricken and apologetic. "We didn't mean to interrupt," she said, grabbing Lewis's shoulder as if to propel him away.

"A little therapeutic touch in the dark?" Gabriel asked blandly.

Sick dismay swept through Kaitlyn. The discovery, the wonder, in Rob's face was shattered. It had been so fragile, something that was about to be born rather than something that already existed—and now it was gone. Snatched away, leaving only Rob's usual kindness and concern. His affection for Anna and Lewis.

And his hatred for Gabriel.

"Kait had a headache," he said, standing up to face Gabriel directly. "If it's any of your business."

"She seems to be better now," Gabriel observed, looking around him at Kaitlyn. Kaitlyn glared at him with deadly heat.

"It would help if people would leave me alone," she said.

"We were just going," Anna said, her eyes telegraphing her contrition to Kaitlyn. "Come on, Lewis."

"That's right," Rob said, and then, to Kait's utter frustration and disbelief, he walked out the door himself. "Want me to close this?" he asked.

If it had been a ploy to make sure Gabriel and the others stayed away, Kaitlyn would have understood. But it wasn't. Rob had reverted completely. The only emotion she could see in his golden eyes now was brotherly affection.

And there was no way to get through to him, no way to change things back. At least for today, it was over.

She didn't know who to be angry with—Gabriel and the others or Rob himself. She might just kill Rob—but she loved him more than ever.

"Yes, please close the door," she said.

When they were all gone, Kaitlyn lay on her bed, watching as cool violet twilight replaced the warm light of afternoon. The room became shadowy, mysterious. She shut her eyes.

A sound alerted her—a sound like paper rustling. Sitting up quickly, she stared around the room. There it was, something white glimmering out of the shadows, creeping in under the door. No, not creeping— being *pushed*.

Kaitlyn quietly got off the bed and padded to the door. Yellow light from the hallway was shining through the crack beneath the door—and the paper was still moving. She ignored it, grabbed the doorknob, and yanked the door open.

Marisol was kneeling on the hallway floor.

The older girl's chin jerked up, and for a moment her brown eyes met Kaitlyn's. They looked shocked and surly. Then she was on her feet and heading for the stairs.

"Oh, no, you don't!" Fired by all the emotions of the past afternoon, Kait pounced. Frustration, excitement, and fury gave her the strength to seize Marisol and spin her around.

"What were you doing pushing stuff under my door? What *is* that?" Kaitlyn demanded, pointing to the piece of folded paper lying on the threshold.

Marisol just tossed her hair out of her eyes and looked defiant.

Kaitlyn let go of her long enough to pick up the paper, then blocked her as she headed for the stairway again.

"This is my picture!" It was the one Kait had done yesterday, the one of her own face with the extra eye, the one she'd left on the lab floor.

Except that now it had writing on it.

Scrawled across the bottom in heavy black pen were the words: WATCH OUT. THIS COULD HAPPEN TO YOU.

"Another joke?" Kaitlyn said grimly, drawing herself up.

Marisol, who was several inches taller, just looked down at her with smoldering brown eyes. Kaitlyn, reckless of the consequences, grabbed Marisol's arm and *shook* her.

"Why are you trying to scare me? Is it because you hate psychics?"

Marisol laughed shortly.

"Do you want me to go *away?* Is it . . . oh, I don't know, some jealousy thing or something?" Kaitlyn was desperately groping for a reason that made sense.

Marisol pressed her full lips together.

"Okay, fine," Kaitlyn said, her voice slightly shaky. "I guess I'll just have to go and ask Joyce."

She got halfway to the stairs before Marisol spoke.

"Joyce can't help you. She doesn't know what's really going on. She wasn't around for the pilot study—but I was."

"What's a pilot study?" Kaitlyn asked, without turning.

118

"Never mind. The point is, you won't get help from Joyce. All she cares about is getting her experiments done, getting her name in the journals. She's blind to what's really happening. That's why Zetes hired her."

"But what does this thing *mean?*" Kaitlyn asked, shaking the paper.

Silence. Kaitlyn turned around. More silence.

"God, you're dumb," Marisol said at last. "Don't you remember the experiment today? Didn't you wonder at all how you got that picture of the grapes?"

Kaitlyn remembered that kaleidoscopic flood of images. "I assume because I'm psychic," she said, but she could hear the stiff defensiveness in her own voice.

"If you were *really* psychic, you'd figure out why you're here. And then you'd be on the next plane home."

Kaitlyn had had it with innuendo. "What are you *talking* about? Why can't you say something straight instead of all this secret stuff?" she almost shouted. "Unless you don't really have anything to say—"

Marisol had flinched at the volume of Kaitlyn's voice—and now she suddenly shoved past her, elbowing Kait hard in the arm. As she reached the stairway, she glanced back and snapped, "I came up to tell you you're late for dinner."

Kaitlyn sagged against the wall.

This had been the most confusing roller coaster of a day . . . and Marisol seemed to be *crazy,* that was all. Except that didn't explain what had happened during Kait's experiment. When Joyce had put that "electrode" on Kaitlyn's forehead . . .

Over my third eye, Kait thought. She looked at the now crumpled paper. The extra eye in the picture stared up at her grotesquely, as if trying to tell her something.

I've got to talk to somebody. I can't deal with this alone. I need *help*.

The decision made her feel better. Kaitlyn wadded the paper up and stuck it in her pocket. Then she hurried down the stairs to dinner.


"What's it got to do with me?" Gabriel said, flicking the paper back toward Kaitlyn. He was lying on his bed reading a magazine about cars—expensive cars. "It's not my problem."

Kaitlyn caught the paper in midair. It had taken a great deal of control to come here. She probably wouldn't have done it except that she couldn't face Rob alone just now, and Anna had been on the phone with her family since dinner.

Grimly Kaitlyn held on to her precarious calm.

"If there's anything to what Marisol is saying, then it's *everybody's* problem," she told Gabriel tightly. "And *you* were the one who said that there was something wrong here."

Gabriel shrugged. "What if I did?"

Kaitlyn felt like screaming. "You really think something's wrong—but you don't care about finding *out?* You wouldn't want to *do* anything about it?"

A faint smile touched Gabriel's lips. "Of course I'm going to do something. I'm going to do what I do best."

Kaitlyn saw it coming, but couldn't avoid feeding him the straight line. Feeling like Sergeant Joe Friday at the end of a scene, she rapped out, "And what's that?"

"Taking care of myself," Gabriel said smugly. His dark eyes were full of wicked delight at having the last word.

Kaitlyn didn't bother to hide her disgust as she left.

Outside his door, she leaned against the wall again. Lewis was in the study playing Primal Scream's newest CD at tooth-vibrating levels. Anna was still in the bedroom on the phone. And as for Rob . . .

"Did the headache come back?"

Kaitlyn whirled, somehow feeling cornered against the wall. Why didn't she ever hear Rob coming?

"No," she said. "I'm fine. At least . . . No, I *am* fine." She couldn't deal with Rob right now, she really couldn't. She was afraid for him—afraid of what she might do to him if she got the chance. It seemed equally likely that she'd kiss him or kill him.

"What's that?" he said, and the next thing Kait knew, he was taking the paper out of her hand. She tried to snatch it back, but he was too fast.

"That's nothing—I mean—"

Rob smoothed the paper, glanced at it, then looked up at her sharply. "Did *you* draw this?"

"Yes . . . but I didn't do the writing. I don't— Oh, it's all so confusing." Kaitlyn had come to the end of her resources. She was tired of fighting, of pushing, of badgering people. She was *tired.*

"Come on," Rob said gently. The hand that cupped her elbow was gentle, too, but irresistible. He guided her without hesitation to the one room on the second floor that wasn't occupied—the bedroom he and Lewis shared.

"Now, tell me all about it." He sat beside her on the bed, as naturally as if he were her brother, as close as that. And with as little ulterior motive. It was agonizing—and wonderful at the same time.

And his eyes—he was looking at her with those grave golden eyes, extraordinary eyes. *Wise* eyes.

I can trust him, Kait thought. No matter what else happens between us, I can trust him.

"It's Marisol," she said, and then she was telling him everything. About waking up that first night to find Marisol in her room, about the strange things Marisol had said. *Watch out or get out. This place is different than you think.* About Marisol claiming it was all a joke the next morning. About the experiment today, and how the pictures had come into her mind—after Joyce put the cold thing on her forehead. About Marisol pushing the drawing under her door.

"And then I tried to get her to explain—but all she talked about was some pilot study, and how if I knew why I was *really* here, I would be on the next plane home. And how Joyce didn't know what was really going on, either."

She stopped. She half expected Rob to laugh, but he didn't. He was frowning, looking puzzled and intent.

"If Joyce doesn't know what's going on, then who does?"

"I guess Mr. Zetes. But, Rob, it's all so crazy."

Rob's mouth tightened. "Maybe," he said under his breath. "But I wondered about him. . . ."

"That first day? The speech about us psychics being so superior and following different laws?"

Rob nodded. Kaitlyn was meeting his eyes without self-consciousness now, as grim as he was. He believed her, and that made this whole thing much more serious than before. This was *business*.

"And why he brought Gabriel here," Rob said.

"Yes," Kaitlyn said slowly. Someday she really would have to talk to Rob about Gabriel—but not now. "But what does it all add up to?"

"I don't know." Rob looked at the drawing again. "But I know we have to find out. We have to talk to Joyce."

Kaitlyn swallowed. It had been a lot easier to threaten to tell Joyce in the heat of anger than it was to consider going to her now. But of course, Rob was right.

"Let's do it," she said.

Joyce's room was off the little wood-paneled hallway under the stairs that led to the front lab. It had originally been a solarium, a glass-enclosed porch. Not only that, but the French-door entrance was so large that anyone in the living room or foyer could see straight in. Only Joyce, Kait thought, could live in a room like this without any privacy. It probably had something to do with the fact that Joyce *always* looked good, whether she was doing business in a tailored suit or lounging in layered pink sweats—like tonight.

"Hi, guys," she said, looking up from a laptop computer. Light from her bedside lamp reflected off the glass walls.

Kaitlyn sat gingerly on the bed, and Rob pulled up the desk chair. He was still holding the drawing.

Joyce looked from one of them to the other. "Why so serious?"

Kaitlyn took a deep breath at the same time as Rob said, "We need to talk to you."

"Yes?"

Kait and Rob exchanged glances. Then Kaitlyn burst out, "It's about Marisol."

Joyce's eyebrows lifted toward her sleek blond hair. "Yes?"

"She's been saying things to Kaitlyn," Rob said. "Weird things, about the Institute being dangerous. And she wrote . . . this . . . on a drawing Kaitlyn did."

Still looking puzzled, Joyce took the paper, scanned it. Kait felt her stomach knot. She had stopped breathing completely.

When Joyce threw back her head, Kait thought for a moment she was going to scream. Instead, she burst into laughter.

Peals of laughter, musical and uncontrollable. After a minute she calmed down into snorts, but when she looked at Kaitlyn and Rob, she went off again.

Kaitlyn felt her own mouth stretch into a smile, but it was the polite, unhappy smile of someone waiting to be let in on a joke. At last Joyce collapsed against the mounded pillows, wiping tears from her eyes.

"I'm sorry . . . it's not really funny. It's just . . . it's her medication. She must not be taking it."

"Marisol takes medication?" Rob asked.

"Yes. And she's fine when she *does* take it; it's just that sometimes she forgets or decides she doesn't need it, and then . . . well. You see." Joyce waved the paper. "I suppose she means it symbolically. She's always been a little worried about psychics misusing their powers." Joyce turned to Kaitlyn, obviously struggling not to grin. "You didn't take her *literally,* I hope?"

Kaitlyn wanted to drop through the floor.

How could she have been so stupid? Of course, it had all been a terrible mistake—she should have realized that. And now she'd blundered in on Marisol's emotional problems, or mental problems, or whatever.

"I'm sorry," she gasped.

Joyce waved a hand, biting her lip to keep from laughing. "Oh, look."

"No, I'm really sorry. It was just—it was kind of spooky, and I didn't understand. . . . I *thought* there must be some simple explanation, but . . ." Kaitlyn took a breath. "Oh, God, I hope we haven't gotten her into trouble."

"No—but maybe I should let Mr. Zetes in on this," Joyce said, sobering. "He was the one who recruited her; she was actually hired before I was. I think she's a friend of his daughter's."

Mr. Zetes had a daughter? She must be pretty old, Kaitlyn thought. It was surprising she would have a friend as young as Marisol.

"Anyway, don't worry about it," Joyce said. "I'll talk to Marisol about her meds tomorrow and get everything straightened out. By the way, Kait, when did you draw this?"

"Oh—yesterday, during the remote viewing experiment. I dropped it when I heard that guy with the Mohawk screaming."

"How is that guy?" Rob asked softly. He was looking at Joyce with steady golden eyes.

"He's fine," Joyce said, and Kaitlyn thought she sounded slightly defensive. "The hospital gave him a tranquilizer and released him."

"Because," Rob went on, "I still think you should be careful with Ga—"

"Yes, right. I'm going to change the protocol with Gabriel's experiment." Joyce's tone closed the subject and she glanced at her clock.

"I'm so embarrassed," Kaitlyn said as she and Rob walked back up the stairs.

"Why? After what Marisol did, you had every right to ask what was going on."

It was true, but Kait still felt that somehow she should have realized. She should have more faith in Mr. Zetes, who, after all, had paid a lot of money to give the five of them a new life. She should have *known* that Marisol was having paranoid delusions.

The new life felt a bit lonely as Kait and Rob parted in the hallway. It was maddening to have him say good night so cheerfully, as if he *enjoyed* being her big brother. As if being anything else had never crossed his mind—which, in his view, it probably hadn't. He seemed to have wiped the entire incident this afternoon out of his consciousness.

Anna sat up as Kaitlyn came in the bedroom. "Where've you been?"

"Downstairs." Kaitlyn wanted to talk to Anna, but she was very, very tired. She fumbled in a drawer for her nightgown. "I think I'll go to sleep early—do you mind?"

"Of course not. You're probably still sick," Anna said, instantly solicitous.

Just before falling asleep, Kaitlyn murmured, "Anna? Do you know what a pilot study is?"

"I think it's a kind of practice experiment—you do

it first, before the real experiment. Like a pilot episode for a TV show comes first."

"Oh. Thanks." Kaitlyn was too sleepy to say more. But it occurred to her that maybe Marisol had told the truth about one thing. Marisol had claimed to have been "around for the pilot study," and Joyce had said that Marisol had been recruited before *her*.

The rest was nonsense, though. Like the idea that Joyce had put something weird on her forehead— God, she was glad Rob hadn't mentioned that to Joyce. Joyce would have thought Kaitlyn needed medication, too.

And Rob . . . But she wouldn't think about Rob now. She'd deal with him tomorrow.

All that night she had strange dreams. In one she was on a windswept peninsula, looking out over a cold gray ocean. In another she was with Marisol and a group of strangers. All of them had eyes in their foreheads. Marisol smirked and said, "Think you're so smart? You're growing one, too. The seed's been planted." Then Gabriel appeared and said, "We've got to look out for ourselves. You see what can happen otherwise?"

Kaitlyn did see. Rob had fallen into a deep crevasse and he was shouting for help. Kaitlyn reached out to him, but Gabriel pulled her back, and Rob's voice kept echoing. . . .

All at once she was awake. The room was full of pale morning light, and the shouting was real.

# 10

The shouts were distant and muffled, but unmistakably hysterical. The clock said 6:15 A.M.

Gabriel, Kait thought wildly, jumping out of bed. What has he done now?

Anna was up, too, her long black hair loose. Her eyes were alert, but not panicked. "What is it?"

"I don't know!"

She and Kait spilled out into the hallway without bothering to put on robes. Rob was just emerging from his room, wearing a tattered pair of pajama bottoms. Kait felt a surge of relief that he wasn't the one doing the shouting.

"It's coming from downstairs," he said.

He took the stairs two at a time, with Kait and Anna right behind him. Kait could hear words in the shouting now.

"Help! God! Somebody help! Quick!"

"It's Lewis!" she said.

The three of them swung around through the dining room and into the kitchen. The shouting stopped.

"Oh, *no,*" Anna said.

Lewis was standing by the kitchen sink, panting. There was a sort of heap at his feet, a heap with mahogany-colored hair at one end.

Marisol.

*"What happened?"* Kait gasped. Lewis just shook his head. Rob had dropped to his knees at once, and was gently turning Marisol over. A trembling started in Kait's legs as she saw the face. Under her olive complexion, Marisol looked chalky. Even her lips were pale. Her eyes were open a little, showing slits of white eyeball.

"Did you call nine-one-one?" Anna asked quietly.

"It's no use," Lewis said in a strangled voice. He was braced against the sink for support, looking down. His face, normally sweet and impish, was drawn with horror. "She's dead. I know she's dead."

Waves of chills swept over Kaitlyn. What Rob was moving was now Marisol's *body,* not Marisol. That one word, "dead," made all the difference. Suddenly Kait didn't want to touch . . . *it.* The body.

She knelt by it anyway, and put a hand on its—Marisol's—chest. Then she jumped a little.

"I think she's breathing."

"She's not dead," Rob said positively. His eyes were shut, his fingers at Marisol's temples. "Her life force is really low, but she's alive. I'm going to try to help." He stopped talking and sat still, his face lined with concentration.

In the background, Kait could hear Anna calling 911.

"What *happened,* Lewis?" she demanded again.

"She had a sort of . . . It looked like a seizure. I came down early because I was hungry, and she was in here cutting up grapefruits, and I said hi, and she was kind of crabby, and then all of a sudden she fell down." Lewis swallowed and blinked rapidly. "I tried to pick her up, but she just kept jerking and shaking. And then she stopped moving. I thought she was dead."

Medication, Kait thought. If Marisol had been on medication for seizures—and she stopped taking it . . . Or for diabetes. Could diabetes give you seizures?

"Where's Joyce?" she said, getting up suddenly. It was the first question she should have asked. Joyce was always down here before the kids, drinking mugs of black coffee and helping Marisol make breakfast.

"Here's a note on the fridge," Anna said. Underneath a magnet shaped like a strawberry was a note in spiky, casual handwriting.

Marisol—
   Coffee filters you bought ystdy *wrong kind.* I'm going to exchange. Start bkfst—cut 3 grapefruit, make muffins. Muff mix in blue bowl in fridge. Where did you put receipt?
                                                    —J

"She's at the store," Kait said, and at that moment heard the front door open.

"Joyce!" She and Lewis shouted it together. Kaitlyn rushed to the dining room entrance. "Joyce, something's happened to Marisol!"

Joyce came running. When she saw Marisol on the floor, she dumped her ecological cloth grocery bag on the counter, where several apples and a box of coffee filters spilled out.

"Oh, my God—what happened?" she said sharply. "Is she breathing all right?" Her hands flew from Marisol's wrist to her neck, searching for a pulse.

Rob didn't answer. He was sitting lotus style by Marisol's head, eyes shut, fingers on her temples. Early sun slanted in the east window and shone on his tanned shoulders.

"I think she's breathing okay now," Lewis whispered. "He said he would try to help her."

Joyce looked hard at Rob, then the strain in her face eased. "Good," she said.

"Is she epileptic?" Kaitlyn asked softly but urgently. "Because Lewis said she had a seizure."

"What? No." Joyce spoke absently. "Oh—you mean the medication? No, it's for something else entirely; he said a psychiatrist prescribed it. God knows, maybe she took an overdose. I never even got to talk to her about it."

"I know. We saw your note," Kait began. "But—"

"Listen—sirens," Anna said.

After that, things happened very quickly. Kait and Anna ran to the front door to wave down the paramedics. Just as the rescue van arrived, a black limousine pulled up behind it. Mr. Zetes got out.

And then there was a lot of confusion. Mr. Z was walking very quickly, despite his cane—and the paramedics were rushing inside with equipment—and the rottweilers were barking—and Kait was behind everyone, trying to see into the kitchen. The noise was deafening.

"Get those dogs out!" one of the paramedics shouted.

Mr. Zetes snapped an order and the dogs backed into the dining room.

"Clear this room!" another paramedic said. She was pulling at Rob, trying to get him away from Marisol. Rob was resisting.

Then Mr. Zetes spoke, in a voice that quieted everyone. "All you young people—go upstairs. You, too, Rob. We'll let the professionals take care of this."

"Sir, she's barely hanging on—" Rob began, his voice thick with worry.

"Move!" the pulling paramedic shouted. Rob moved.

On her way up the stairs, Kait came face-to-face with Gabriel, who was coming down.

"They don't want us," she said. "Go back up. How come it took you so long, anyway?"

"I never get up until seven," Gabriel murmured, backing up. He was fully dressed.

"Didn't you hear the yelling?"

"It was hard to ignore, but I managed."

Rob glared at him as he passed. Gabriel returned it with a derisive look that started with Rob's bare feet and ended with Rob's tousled head.

"We can see from the study window," Lewis said, and they all followed him into the alcove—except Gabriel, who went to one of the other windows.

In a few moments the paramedics came out with a stretcher. Lewis's hand made a slight movement toward his camera, which was lying on the window seat. Then it dropped to his side again.

They all watched as the stretcher was loaded into the back of the paramedics' van. Kait felt both frightened and strangely remorseful. Marisol's face had looked so small among all the big rescue workers and the equipment.

"I hope she's all right. She's got to be all right," she said, and then she sat down on the window seat. Her legs were very shaky.

Anna sat down and put an arm around her. "At least Joyce is going, too," she said in her quiet, gentle voice. A little of her calm penetrated Kaitlyn, like a cool wind blowing. Below, Joyce climbed into the van and it pulled out. The black limo stayed.

Rob was leaning against the window glass, one knee on the seat beside Kait. He was completely unself-conscious about his lack of dress.

"Mr. Z sure does have bad luck," he said softly. "Every time he comes here, he finds trouble."

The cool wind blowing through Kaitlyn turned cold. She looked quickly at Rob. "What are you saying?"

"Nothing," he said, still gazing out the window. "It's just too bad for him, that's all."

Lewis and Anna looked puzzled. Kait stared down at the black limousine, feeling an uneasy stirring in her stomach.

After a while, Mr. Zetes called them down to go to school. Nobody wanted breakfast. Kait didn't want to go to school, either, but Mr. Zetes didn't ask her opinion. He escorted them out to the limousine and ordered the driver to take them.

"Oh, God, I left my sociology book," Kait said when they reached the corner. The limousine, instead of turning around, backed up.

Kait ran up the porch steps and yanked the door open, conscious of the five people waiting on her in the car. She burst inside—and then stopped in middash. Mr. Z's two rottweilers were running toward her, toenails clacking and skidding on the hardwood floor. A terrible baying struck her with the force of a physical blow.

Kaitlyn had never been afraid of a dog in her life—but these weren't dogs, they were salivating monsters whose barking made the ceiling ring. She could see their pink and black gums.

She looked around desperately for a weapon—and saw Mr. Zetes.

He was standing in the little hallway just in front of Joyce's room. The strange thing was that Kaitlyn hadn't seen him arrive—and she was sure he hadn't been there when she burst in. She'd been looking in that direction, because that was where the dogs had come from.

Even stranger, she would have sworn that no door had opened or closed over there. The door to the front lab, just behind him, was shut. So were the French doors to his left—the ones that opened on Joyce's room.

But there *wasn't* any other door—to Mr. Z's right was only a solid wall that supported the staircase. So he *had* to have come from the lab or Joyce's room.

Kait saw his mouth move, and the dogs shut up. He

gave her a courtly nod, his piercing dark eyes on her face.

"I forgot my sociology book," Kaitlyn said unsteadily. Her pulse was hammering, and for some reason she felt as if she were being caught in a lie.

"I see. Run up and get it," was all he said, but he waited until she came downstairs with it, and saw her out the door.

The drawing came, appropriately, during art studio class.

Kaitlyn had been thinking about Mr. Zetes all day, and had made the interesting discovery that it's quite possible to be miserable during lunch even though important people are being nice to you. Several cheerleaders and three or four attractive guys had sat down to talk to her group—but it didn't matter. However Kaitlyn tried to listen to them, her mind kept drifting to Mr. Zetes standing in that cul-de-sac of a hallway. Like a magician appearing in a sealed cabinet.

In art class, Kaitlyn was supposed to be doing a project for her portfolio—that important collection of pictures that might get her college credit next year—but she couldn't focus. The busy, creative classroom around her was only a blur and a hum.

Almost mesmerized, she flipped to a blank page in her sketchbook and reached for her oil pastels.

She loved pastels because they made it so easy to get what she saw from her eyes to the paper. They were quick, fluid, vigorous—free. For a normal picture, she would start by rapidly sketching the major shapes, then layering on detail. But for the *other* kind of picture, the kind she didn't control . . .

She watched her hand dot tiny strokes of carmine and crimson lake in a rectangular shape. A tall rectangle. Around the rectangle, strokes of Van Dyke brown and burnt umber. The close dots of the browns gradually formed a shimmering pattern, with whorls and lines like wood grain.

Her hand hesitated over the box of pastels—what color next? After a moment she picked up black.

Black strokes clustered heavily inside the rectangle, forming a shape. A human silhouette, with broad shoulders and body lines that swept straight down. Like a coat. A man in a coat.

Kaitlyn sat back and looked at the drawing.

She recognized it. It was one of the images she'd seen in that visionary mosaic yesterday—the doorway. Only now she could see the full picture.

A man in a coat in front of the rectangle of an open door. The red of the doorway gave an impression of energy around him. Framing the door was wood—wood paneling.

The solid wall across from Joyce's door was wood-paneled.

"Nice broken color technique," a voice above her said. "Do you need a squirt of fixative?"

Kaitlyn shook her head and the teacher moved on.

The limousine picked them up after school. Joyce was still at the hospital, Mr. Zetes told them when they got home. Marisol was still unconscious. There wouldn't be any testing today.

Kait waited until everyone had drifted upstairs, and then quietly, one by one, she began to gather them.

"We've got to talk. In the study," she said. Anna,

Lewis, and Rob all came at once. Gabriel came when she stuck her head in his room and hissed at him.

When they were together in the study, she shut the door and turned the TV on. Then she showed them the picture and told them what she'd seen that morning.

"So you think, like . . . what? There's really a door there?" Lewis asked. "But what does that *mean?* I mean, so what?"

Kaitlyn looked at Rob, whose eyes were dark, dark gold.

"There's more," she said, and she told Anna and Lewis what she'd told Rob and Gabriel the night before. All of it, about Marisol's warnings and the strange things that had been happening.

When she was through, there was no sound except the blaring of a music video on TV.

Anna sat with her head slightly tilted, her long braid falling into her lap, her eyes faraway and sad. Lewis rubbed his nose, forehead puckered. Rob's face was set, his fists resting on his knees. Kaitlyn herself gripped the sides of her sketchbook tensely.

Gabriel was sitting back with one knee hooked over the arm of the couch. He was playing with a quarter, flipping it over and catching it. He seemed completely unconcerned.

Finally Anna said, *"Something's* going on. Any one of those things—like what Marisol said, or the cold thing on your forehead—any one of them could be explained. But when you put them all together, something's . . ."

"Amiss," Rob supplied.

"Amiss," Anna said.

Lewis's face cleared. "But look. If you think there's a door down there, why don't we just go down and *see?*"

"We can't," Anna said. "Mr. Z's in the living room, and so are the dogs."

"He's got to leave sometime," Rob said.

Lewis squirmed. "Look—you're really saying that the Institute is, like, evil? You really think so?" He turned to Rob. "I thought you loved this place, the whole idea of it."

Gabriel snorted. Rob ignored him. "I do love the idea of it," he said. "But the reality . . . I've just got a bad feeling about it. And Kait does, too."

Everyone looked at Kait, who hesitated. "I don't know about feelings," she said finally, looking down at the picture of a door. "I don't even know whether to trust my drawings. But there's only one way to find out about this one."

It took them half an hour to plan the burglary. Actually, it only took five minutes to do the planning. The other twenty-five were spent trying to force Gabriel to help.

"No, thanks. Include me out," he said.

"You wouldn't have to go inside," Kaitlyn said through her teeth. "All you need to do is sit in the alcove and watch for cars coming in the driveway."

Gabriel shook his head.

Anna tried gentle reasoning with him; Lewis tried bribery. None of it worked.

At last Rob stood up with an exclamation of disgust and turned toward the door. "Stop catering to him. He's afraid. It doesn't matter; we can do it without him."

138

Gabriel's eyes went hard. "Afraid?"

Rob barely glanced back at him. "Yeah."

Gabriel stood up. "Care to say that again?"

This time Rob turned. He stood face-to-face with Gabriel and their eyes locked, silently fighting it out.

Kaitlyn watched them both without breathing. Thinking again that they were so different, such opposites. Rob all gold, radiant energy, his waving hair tousled, his eyes blazing. And Gabriel darkness, his skin paler than usual, his hair looking black in contrast. His eyes bottomless and cold.

Like the sun and a black hole, side by side, Kait thought. In that moment the image was etched into her mind, a picture she would never draw. It was too frightening.

Once again, she was afraid for Rob. She knew what Gabriel could do—with or without a knife. If they started fighting . . .

"I'm going downstairs," she said abruptly. "To ask Mr. Z if we can order a pizza."

Everyone looked at her, startled. Then Kait saw understanding flash in Anna's eyes.

"That's a good idea. I'm sure nobody wants to cook dinner," Anna said, standing and gently taking Rob's elbow. She nudged Lewis with her foot.

"Uh, fine with me," Lewis said, putting his baseball cap on backward. He was still looking at Gabriel.

Slowly, to Kaitlyn's great relief, the two combatants broke their locked stare and stepped away from each other. Rob submitted to Anna's gentle tugging. Kaitlyn made sure he got out the door.

Then she looked back at Gabriel.

His eyes were still dark as black holes, but his

139

mouth was mocking and sardonic. "You can put it off, but it's going to happen someday," he said. Before Kaitlyn could defiantly ask *what* was going to happen, he added, "I'll watch for cars up here. But that's all. I won't risk my neck to help you. If something goes wrong, you're on your own."

Kaitlyn shrugged. "I've always been on my own," she said, and went downstairs to order pizza.

Mr. Zetes didn't leave until eleven o'clock. Kaitlyn was afraid to have the group stay downstairs with him after dinner, afraid that one of them might give something away. They sat in the study, pretending to do homework, and all the time listening for a sign that Mr. Z was going.

When he finally did go, he called them to the staircase and said that Joyce would undoubtedly be coming soon.

"But you won't be alone until then. I'll leave Prince and Baron," he said.

Kaitlyn studied his face, wondering how much he suspected they suspected. Were those dark eyes fierce or just acute? Was there the shadow of a grim smile on his lips?

He can't *know* anything, she thought.

Acting for all she was worth, she said, "Oh, thank you, Mr. Zetes."

When the front door shut behind him, Kaitlyn looked at Anna, who looked back helplessly.

"Prince and Baron?" Kait said.

Anna sighed, fingering the end of her black braid. In anyone else it would have been a nervous gesture. "I don't know. I *will* try, but they look very hard to influence."

"You'd better go if you're going," Gabriel said curtly.

"You just go hide—I mean *stand guard*—in the dark," Rob said. Kaitlyn grabbed his wrist and dragged him a step or two down the stairs. Dearly as she loved Rob, there were times when she wanted to bash his head in.

Gabriel retreated into the darkened study, his handsome face inscrutable.

"You first, Anna," Kaitlyn said. Anna walked down the stairs, so slowly and gracefully that she might have been drifting. Rob and Kait followed, with Lewis behind.

"Careful. Easy," Anna said as she reached the bottom. A low growl sounded from somewhere behind the staircase.

One dog was in the paneled hallway, Kaitlyn saw as they rounded the corner. The other was in the darkened living room, almost blending into the shadows. Both were watching Anna intently.

"Easy," Anna breathed, and that was the last word she said. She stood perfectly still, looking at the dog in the living room, her left hand raised toward the dog in the hallway, the way you'd gesture to a person to wait.

The growl died away. Anna's upraised hand slowly closed, as if she'd caught something in her fist. She turned, smoothly and without haste, to look at the dog in the hallway.

"Look out!" Rob yelled, jumping forward.

In absolute silence, with its lips peeled back and the hair on its back bristling, the dog in the living room was stalking toward Anna.

# 11

Everything happened too quickly for Kaitlyn to take in. She only knew that she grabbed desperately for Rob's arm to hold him back, thinking that only Anna could deal with the dog, and anyone else was likely to distract her. And then Anna was holding up her hand in a commanding gesture—*stop*—but the dog was still coming. Moving eerily, as if on oiled machinery, every tooth showing.

*"No!"* Anna said sharply, and added some words in a language Kaitlyn didn't know. "Hwhee, Sokwa! Brother Wolf—go to sleep! It's not hunting time now. Rest and sleep."

Then, without showing the slightest sign of fear, she reached for the snarling muzzle. She locked one hand over it, grabbing the hair at the dog's neck with the other. Her eyes gazed straight into the animal's, unflinching and unwavering.

"I'm the pack leader here," she said clearly. "This is not your territory. I am dominant." Kaitlyn had the

142

feeling that the words were only part of the communication. Something unspoken was passing between the graceful girl and the animal.

And the dog was responding. His lips slid down to cover his teeth again. The hair on his back flattened. More—his entire back flattened, drooped, until his belly almost touched the floor. His tail tucked between his legs. His eyes shifted. His entire attitude was one of submission.

Anna held out a hand to the other dog, which moved toward her slowly, tail down, almost crawling on its elbows. She clamped a hand over its muzzle, clearly establishing dominance.

Rob's eyebrows were up. "How long can you sustain that?"

"I don't know," Anna said without turning. "I'll try to keep them right here—but you guys had better work fast." She tilted her head and, still looking at the dogs, began chanting something softly. Kaitlyn didn't understand the words, but the rhythm was soothing. The dogs seemed mesmerized, cringing a little, pushing at her gently with their noses.

"Let's go," Rob said.

The paneling in the hallway was dark—walnut or mahogany, Kaitlyn thought vaguely. She and Rob both scanned it intently, while Lewis squinted doubtfully.

"There," she said, pointing to the middle panel. "That looks like a crack, doesn't it? It could be the top of a door."

"That means there must be a release somewhere around here," Rob said, running his fingers over the smooth wood and into the grooves between panels.

"But we'll probably never find it by accident. You may have to push more than one place, and do it in a certain sequence or something."

"Okay, Lewis," Kait said. "Do your stuff."

Lewis edged between them, muttering, "But I don't know what *to* do. I don't know anything about secret doors."

"You don't know exactly what you're doing when you use PK on the random number machine, either, do you?" Kaitlyn demanded. "So how do you manage that?"

"I just kind of . . . nudge at the thing with my mind. It's not conscious. I just nudge and see what happens, and if something works, I keep doing it."

"Like biofeedback," Rob said. "People don't know *how* they slow down their heart rate, but they do."

"Well, nudge this panel and see what happens," Kait told Lewis. "We've got to find that door—if there is a door."

Lewis began, stroking the panel lightly with outspread fingers. Every so often he would stop and push on the wood, his entire body tense. Kaitlyn knew he was pushing with his mind, too.

"Come on, where are you?" he muttered. "Open, open."

Something clicked.

"Got it!" Lewis said, sounding more astonished than triumphant.

Kaitlyn stared, her knees going weak.

There *was* a door. Or a passage, anyway. The middle panel had recessed and slid smoothly behind the panel on the left. There was a gaping hole in the formerly solid wall.

It looked just like Kaitlyn's drawing, except that there was no figure in the doorway. There were only stairs leading downward, faintly illuminated by half-covered reddish lights at foot level. They seemed to have been activated by the door opening.

Lewis breathed one word. "Jeeeeeez."

"Why is it so dark?" Kait murmured. "Why not put some real lights in?"

Rob nodded toward the French doors to Joyce's room just opposite. "Maybe because *she's* there. This way, you could walk into this place without being seen, even at night."

Kaitlyn frowned, then shrugged. There was no time to wonder about it. "Lewis, you stay up here. If Gabriel yells that he sees lights coming up the driveway, tell us. We'll come up fast, and you can close the door."

"*If* I can close the door," Lewis said. "It's like trying to learn how to wiggle your ears—you don't know how until you do it." But he stationed himself by the panel like a resolute soldier.

"I'll go first," Rob said, and began cautiously making his way down the stairs. Kaitlyn followed, wishing that she'd brought a flashlight. She didn't at all like this journey into red-hazed dimness—although the lights illuminated the steps themselves, they showed nothing around them. The stairway seemed suspended in an abyss.

"Here's the bottom," Rob said. "It feels like another hallway—wait, here's a switch."

Light blossomed, cool, greenish fluorescent light. They were in a short hallway. The only door was at the end.

"We may need Lewis again," Kaitlyn said, but the door opened when Rob turned the handle.

Kaitlyn didn't know what she expected to see, but it certainly wasn't what she saw. An ordinary office, with a corner desk and a computer and filing cabinets. After the sliding panel and the dark staircase, it was something of a letdown.

She looked at Rob. "You don't think . . . I mean, what if we're completely wrong here? What if he just has a hidden room because he's eccentric? It's possible."

"Anything's possible," Rob said, so shortly that she knew he wondered, too. He went to the filing cabinet and pulled out a drawer with a sliding rattle.

The sound made Kaitlyn's skin jump. If they *were* wrong, they had no business poking into things.

Defiantly she went over to the desk and thumbed through some papers from the letter tray. They were business letters, mostly from important-sounding people, addressed to Mr. Zetes. They all seemed to be photocopies, duplicates. Big deal.

"You know what?" she asked grimly, still pawing. "I just realized. If Mr. Z *was* trying to hide something, he'd never hide it *here*. Why should he? He's got to have better places. He's got a *house*, doesn't he? He's got a *corporation*, somewhere—"

"Kaitlyn."

"Well?"

"I think you should look at this." Rob was holding a file from the cabinet. There was a photograph of Kait clipped on the jacket, and in bold letters: KAITLYN BRADY FAIRCHILD, PROJECT BLACK LIGHTNING.

"What's Project Black Lightning?"

"I don't know. There's a file like that for each of us. Inside there's just a bunch of papers—all kinds of information. Did you know they have your birth certificate?"

"The lawyers told Dad they needed stuff. . . . What's that?"

"A graph about your testing, I think." Rob's tanned finger traced the bottom axis. "Look, this is dated yesterday. It says *First Testing with*—and then there's a word I can't read."

"First testing with something," Kaitlyn repeated slowly. She touched her forehead. "But what does it mean?"

Rob shook his head. "There's another set of files here, with other names." He held up a file jacket with a photo of a smiling girl with dark brown hair. It was labeled SABRINA JESSICA GALLO, BLACK LIGHTNING PILOT STUDY.

Running diagonally across the label, in thick red ink, the word TERMINATED was scrawled.

Kaitlyn and Rob looked at each other.

"Which was terminated?" Kait breathed. "The study or the girl?"

Silently, with one impulse, they turned back to their search.

"Okay, I've got a letter," Kait said after a moment. "It's from the Honorable Susan Baldwin—a judge. It says, 'Enclosed is a list of potential clients who might be interested in the project.' *The project.*" Kaitlyn's eyes scanned down the list. " 'Max Lawrence—up for sentencing May first. TRI-Tech, Inc.—settlement conference with Clifford Electronics Limited, June twenty-fourth.' It's all like that, names and trial dates and stuff."

"Here's another file," Rob said. "It's hard to figure out, but I think it's an old grant from NASA. Yeah, a grant from NASA for half a million, back in eighty-six. For"—he paused and read carefully—"investigation into the feasibility of the development of psychoactive weaponry."

"What of the what?" Kaitlyn said hopelessly. "Psycho-*what?*"

Rob's eyes were dark gold and bleak.

"I don't know what it all adds up to. But it's not good. There's a *lot* Mr. Z didn't tell us."

"'This place is different than you think,'" Kaitlyn quoted. "And there *was* a pilot study before us—so Marisol told the truth. But what happened to those kids? What happened to Sabrina?"

"And what's going to happen to—" Rob broke off. "Did you hear that? A noise up there?"

Kaitlyn listened, but she didn't hear anything.

Upstairs, Gabriel was seething.

The whole plan was stupid, of course. Why did they want to go meddling in what was obviously not their business? The time to worry about Zetes was when he was trying to *do* something to you, not before. Then fight—kill him, if necessary. He was only an old man. But why ruin what had so far proved to be a very comfortable deal?

It was all *his* idea, Gabriel felt sure. Kessler's. Rob the Virtuous probably felt there was something un-

148

spiritual about coming into so much money. He had to wreck it somehow.

And Kaitlyn was just as bad these days. Completely under Kessler's spell. Why should Gabriel care about her, a girl who was in love with a guy he hated? A girl who only disturbed him . . .

*A girl with hair like fire and witch eyes,* his mind whispered.

A girl who hounded him, badgered him . . .

*Who challenges you,* his mind whispered. *Who could be your equal.*

A girl who interfered with him, trying to get inside his guard . . .

*Whose spirit is like yours.*

Oh, shut up, Gabriel told his brain, and stared broodingly into the darkness beyond the study window.

The street in front of the Institute was silent and deserted. Naturally, it was midnight—and here in the suburbs that meant everyone was tucked nice and snug in their beds.

Nevertheless, Gabriel felt uneasy. Little sounds seemed to be nagging at his subconscious. Cars on the streets behind the Institute, probably.

Cars . . . Suddenly Gabriel stiffened. Eyes narrowed, he listened for a moment, then he left the alcove.

Nothing out the west window of the study. With the silent steps of a housebreaker he headed for the back of the house, to Rob and Lewis's bedroom. He looked out the back window, the one facing north.

And there it was. The limo. It had obviously come

up the narrow dirt road in back. Now the only question was whether Zetes was just about to get out, or—

Directly beneath him, in the kitchen, Gabriel heard a door open.

The back door, he thought. And those idiots downstairs are all waiting for him to come from the front.

There wasn't any time to go down and warn them—and Zetes would hear a shout.

Gabriel's lip curled. Tough. Kaitlyn knew the truth. He'd told her he wouldn't risk his neck for her. Not that there was anything he could do anyway, except . . .

He shook his head slightly. Not that. In the darkened window his reflected eyes were cold and hard.

Below, the kitchen door slammed.

No, he told himself. He wouldn't. He wouldn't . . .

On the bottom of the letter tray was a scribbled page like something you might doodle while on the telephone. Kaitlyn could make out the scrawled words "Operation Lightning Strike" and "psychic strike team."

"This is weird—" she began. She never finished the sentence because *it* hit her.

Just what *it* was, she couldn't tell at first. Like Rob's healing transfusion of energy, it wasn't something you could see or hear or taste. But while Rob's energy flow had been wonderful, invigorating, an intense pleasure, this was like being hit by a runaway train. Kaitlyn had the feeling of being violated.

And while it didn't trigger any of her normal senses, it mimicked them. Kaitlyn smelled roses. She felt a burning in her head—a painful searing that built until a light like one of Lewis's flashbulbs went off in her brain. Then, through the explosion, she heard a voice.

Gabriel's voice.

*Get out of there! He just came in the back door!*

For a moment Kait stood paralyzed. Knowing that Gabriel could communicate directly with her mind was very different from *feeling* it. Her first reaction was that she was hallucinating; it was impossible.

Rob was gasping. "God. He's a telepath."

*Shut up, Kessler. Move. Do something. You're about to get caught.*

Kaitlyn felt another wave of astonishment. The communication was two-way—Gabriel could hear Rob. Then some primitive instinct within her awoke and shoved all speculation aside. This wasn't the time to think—it was time to *act*.

She threw the letters back in the tray and slid the drawers of the file cabinet shut. Then she had an idea and she tried to do something she'd never done before. She tried to send a thought. She didn't know *how* to send one, but she tried, concentrating on the burning-roses sensation in her head. *Gabriel—can you hear me? You need to tell Anna he's here. Tell her to hang on to the dogs until—*

*I can hear you, Kaitlyn. It's Anna.* The answer was lighter, calmer, than Gabriel's communication. It was a lot like Anna's speaking voice.

Kaitlyn realized something. Not only could she hear Anna, but she had a sense of where Anna was, and what Anna was doing. It was as if she could feel Anna's presence. And Lewis's . . .

*Lewis, shut the panel,* she thought. *And then get upstairs. Anna, let the dogs go as soon as he does.*

*And what are you going to do?* Lewis asked. Kait could sense that he was working on the panel.

*Hide,* Rob said briefly, turning off the fluorescent lights in the hallway and the office.

Although it seemed like hours since the explosion in Kaitlyn's mind, she knew it was only a few seconds. This strange telepathy might be very, very disconcerting, but it was an extraordinarily efficient way to communicate.

*I've got the panel shut. I'm going upstairs,* Lewis said.

*I'm letting the dogs go—quick, Lewis! Come on!* Anna's voice sharpened, and Kait felt a surge of urgency from her.

*What's happening?* Kait demanded.

*Wait—I think it's all right. Yes.* Now what Kait felt from Anna was relief. *He was coming around through the dining room just as we went up the stairs, but I don't think he saw us. He was looking down at the dogs.*

*You two had better get into bed. He might come upstairs,* Rob said. Kaitlyn turned toward him in the dark. It was fascinating—his silent mental voice sounded just like his ordinary voice, but more so. It was more honest, it seemed to carry more of *him* in it. Right now it was full of quiet concern for Anna and Lewis.

"Or he might come down here," Rob's real voice whispered to Kait. "Come on."

He took her hand. How he could navigate in the dark was beyond her, but he guided them both to the corner desk.

"Get under it," he whispered. "The file cabinets block off the view from the door."

Kaitlyn found herself squeezing into a very tight place.

And then they waited. There was nothing else to do. Kaitlyn's heart was beating violently, seeming loud in the quietness. Her hand in Rob's was slick. Sitting still was much harder than moving and talking had been.

Another fear had gripped her. This was Gabriel's power, right? The one that had killed Iris, the girl in Durham; that had driven the Mohawk volunteer crazy after forty-five seconds. How long had Gabriel kept their minds linked up tonight? And how much longer before he started to suck *their* brains out?

It has to get unstable, she reminded herself. That's what he said. He can control it if he keeps the contact short.

She was still afraid. Even though Gabriel hadn't said anything since the beginning, she could *feel* him out there. A strong presence, surrounded by smooth, hard walls. He was keeping them all in contact. And every second that ticked by made the contact more dangerous.

Beside her, Rob stiffened. *Listen*, he said.

Kaitlyn heard. A sliding, rattling sound. The panel.

*I don't think that's Lewis*, Rob said.

*It's not. I'm in bed*, Lewis said.

Anna's mental voice was clear and purposeful. *Do you want us to do anything, Kait?*

Kait took a deep breath, then sent the thought, *No, just sit tight. We'll be fine.* At the same time she felt Rob squeeze her hand. There were some things that

153

could be said without even telepathy. She and Rob both knew that they wouldn't be fine—but she couldn't think of any way for Anna to help.

Light suddenly showed in a diffuse fan pattern on the office floor. Mr. Zetes had turned on the fluorescents in the hallway.

Please don't let him come in. Please don't let him come in, Kaitlyn thought. Then she tried to stop thinking, in case the others could hear her panic.

The office door was opening, light spilling in.

Beneath the desk, Kaitlyn buried her face in Rob's shoulder, trying to keep absolutely still. If he didn't actually *come* in—if he only looked in . . .

More light. Mr. Z had turned on the office switch. Now he had only to step beyond the file cabinets to see them.

I wonder if we'll be terminated, Kait thought. Like Sabrina. Like Marisol. She wanted to jump out and get it over with, to confront Mr. Zetes. They were lost anyway. The only thing that kept her from moving was Rob's arm around her.

Upstairs, she heard a wild clamor. An explosion of barking and baying.

*What is it?* she thought.

Gabriel's voice, cool sarcasm underlaid with heated anger, came back. *I've riled the dogs a little. I figure that should bring him up.*

Kaitlyn held her breath. There was a pause, then the lights in the office went off and the door shut. A minute later the light in the hallway went off, too—and then she heard a rattle.

She sagged against Rob. He squeezed her with both

arms and she clung back, even though it was really too warm for clinging.

Above, the barking went on and on. Then, gradually, it faded as if getting more distant.

Gabriel's voice came again. *He's taking them out to the limo. I don't think he's coming back, but Joyce might be—any minute now.*

*Lewis,* Rob said, *get us out of here.*

Ten minutes later, they were all upstairs in the study.

It was perfectly dark except for the moonlight coming in the window. They could barely see each other, but that didn't matter. They could *feel* each other.

Kaitlyn had never been so aware of other people in her life. She knew where each of them was; she had a vague sense of what each was doing. It was as if they were not quite separate creatures—isolated and yet attached somehow.

Like insects caught in a huge web, she thought. Tied together by almost invisible threads. Every pull on the strands lets you know someone else is moving. Her artist's mind gave her an image: the five of them hanging trapped, spread-eagled, and the silken strands between them humming with power.

"Nice picture. But I don't want to be trapped in a web with you," Lewis said mildly.

"And I don't want to have you reading my thoughts," Kaitlyn told him. "That was private."

*How am I . . .* "I mean, how am I supposed to tell?" Lewis asked, changing from mental voice to ordinary voice in midsentence.

"Nobody likes it," Rob said. "Switch it off, Gabriel."

There was a silence which Kaitlyn sensed with both mind and ears.

Everyone turned to look at Gabriel. He looked back with cold defiance.

"Fine," he said. "Just tell me how."

# 12

Kaitlyn stared into the darkness where Gabriel was sitting.

*What do you mean?* Rob asked, deadly quiet. He didn't even seem to notice he wasn't speaking out loud.

"What have you done before?" Anna put in quickly. "I mean, how does it stop, usually?"

Gabriel turned to her. "Usually? When people drop dead or start screaming."

There was another blank silence, then a sudden gabble of voices, both mental and otherwise.

*Are you saying it's going to kill us?*—that was Lewis.

"Just a minute; let's all stay calm."—Anna.

*I think you'd better start explaining, buddy!*—Rob.

Gabriel sat for a moment, and Kait had the feeling of raised hackles and bared teeth from him—like one of the rottweilers. Then, slowly and coldly, he began to explain.

It was the story he'd told Kaitlyn about his powers:

157

about how Iris, the girl in Durham, had died, about his escape afterward, about the man who'd tried to kill him, the man he'd killed instead. He told it without emotion—but Kaitlyn could feel the emotion that was suppressed behind the wall. They all could— and Kaitlyn could tell that, too.

*I hate this as much as you do,* Gabriel finished. *The last thing I want is to see what's in your helpless little minds. But if I knew how to control it, I wouldn't be here.*

*He feels more trapped than anyone else. Like a spider caught in its own web,* Anna commented, and Kaitlyn wondered if it was meant to be a shared insight, or if Anna was just thinking it.

"But then why did you do it to *us* tonight?" Rob demanded. Kait could feel the bewilderment emanating from him. Direct contact with Gabriel's mind had shaken his view of Gabriel as a selfish, ruthless killer—Kaitlyn could tell that. Which was funny, she thought, because the image of a selfish, ruthless killer was exactly what Gabriel was trying so hard to project right now. "If you knew you couldn't control it, why did you use telepathy on us?" Rob said angrily.

*Because I couldn't think of any other way to save your useless necks!* Gabriel's reply had the force of a knockout blow.

Rob sat back.

"There probably *wasn't* another way," Kaitlyn said judiciously. "Mr. Zetes was just about to walk in on us when the dogs started barking. What did you do to them, by the way?"

*Threw a shoe at them.*

*At* those *dogs? Jeeeez,* Lewis said.

Gabriel seemed to give a mental shrug. *I figured he'd have to come up and see what was going on. Then he couldn't get them to shut up, so he finally had to take them outside.*

"Look," Anna broke in, "maybe we shouldn't be using this thing so much. Maybe it'll go away sooner if we all just ignore it."

"It'll go away when we go to sleep," Gabriel said flatly—but aloud, Kaitlyn noticed.

"Are you sure?" Lewis asked.

"Yes."

Kaitlyn decided not to mention that Gabriel didn't *feel* as sure as he sounded.

"We really should go to sleep, anyway," she said. It was only now, when all the panic and excitement were over, that she could begin to realize how tired she was. She was stiff from tension and from sitting under that desk. And her mind was exhausted from trying to take in everything that had gone on today. From Marisol's seizure, to Mr. Zetes appearing by the hidden door, to her drawing in art class, to the burglary—so much had happened that her brain was simply giving up.

"But you didn't tell us what was down there behind the panel," Lewis said. "Did you find *anything?*"

"We found plenty, all bad," Rob said. "But Kaitlyn's right. We can talk about it tomorrow."

Kaitlyn could feel Anna biting her lip on questions, judging that it was wiser to wait. She could feel Lewis sighing. But it was all muffled by an enormous sense of weariness—even of dizziness, of illness. She wasn't just feeling her own fatigue, she realized. Gabriel was on the verge of collapse. He was—

*Rob,* she said urgently.

Rob was already moving. In trying to stand up, Gabriel had staggered and fallen to his knees. Kaitlyn helped Rob put him back on the couch.

"He's bad off—like you when you burned up so much energy yesterday, Kait," Rob told her. He was holding Gabriel's arm—and Gabriel was resisting feebly.

"I don't burn energy doing this. I take energy," he said.

"Well, you burned something this time," Rob said. "Maybe because you were connecting so many people. Anyway . . ." Kaitlyn could hear him take a deep breath—and sense him getting a better grip on Gabriel's arm. "Anyway, maybe I can help you. Let me—"

*"No!"* Gabriel shouted. "Let go of me."

"But you need energy. I can—"

*I said, let go!* Once again, the thought itself was an attack. Kaitlyn winced and everyone backed up a little—everyone except Rob. He stood his ground.

Lewis said weakly, "I think he's got enough energy right now."

Gabriel's attention was still on Rob. "I don't need anything from anyone," he snarled, trying to pull out of Rob's grip. "Especially not from you."

"Gabriel, listen—" Kait began. But Gabriel wasn't in a mood to listen. She could feel waves of defensive, destructive fury beating at her like the icy battering of a storm.

*I don't need any of you. This doesn't change anything, so don't think it does. By tomorrow it'll be gone—and until then, just leave me alone!*

Rob hesitated, then released Gabriel's arm. "Whatever you want," he said almost gently. He stepped back.

Now, Kaitlyn thought, comes the interesting part. Whether Gabriel can make it to his room on his own or not.

He did. Not very steadily, but belligerently. Not needing words to send the message that they'd all better keep away.

The door to the large bedroom shut hard behind him. Kaitlyn could still feel his presence on the other side, but it was a feeling of walls, of spiky barriers. She herself used to have walls like that.

"Poor guy," Lewis muttered.

"I think we'd all better go to bed," Anna suggested.

They did. Kaitlyn's clock said 2:52 A.M. She wondered vaguely how they were going to make it to school tomorrow, and then exhaustion overcame her.

The last thing she remembered, as her defenses lowered in sleep, was thinking, *By the way, Gabriel, thanks. For risking your own neck.*

She got only nasty images of icy walls and locked doors as an answer.


She was dreaming, and it was the old dream about the peninsula—the rocky peninsula and the ocean and the cold wind. Kaitlyn shivered in the spray. The sky was so dark with clouds that she couldn't tell if it was day or evening. A single, lonely gull circled over the water.

What a desolate place, she thought.

"Kaitlyn!"

Oh, yes, Kaitlyn remembered. *The voice calling my name; that was in my first dream, too. And now I turn around and there's no one there.*

Feeling resigned, she turned. And started.

Rob was climbing down the rocks. His gold-blond hair was flecked with spray and there was damp sand on his pajama bottoms.

"I don't think you're supposed to be here," Kaitlyn told him with the confused directness of dreams.

"I don't *want* to be here. It's freezing," Rob said, hopping and slapping his bare arms with his hands.

"Well, you should have worn more sensible clothes."

"I'm freezing, too," a third voice said. Kaitlyn looked. Lewis and Anna were behind her, both looking chilled and windswept. "Whose dream is this, anyway?" Lewis added.

"This is a very strange place," Anna said, gazing around with dark, thoughtful eyes. Then she said, "Gabriel—are you all right?"

Gabriel was standing a little way down the peninsula, his arms folded. Kaitlyn felt that this dream was getting crowded—and ridiculous. "It's funny—" she began.

*I don't think it's funny, and I'm not going to play,* Gabriel's voice said in her head.

. . . *if it was a dream.*

Suddenly Kaitlyn was very much in doubt.

"Are you *really* here?" she asked Gabriel. He just looked at her coldly, with eyes the color of the ocean around them.

Kaitlyn turned to the others. "Look, you guys, I've

had this dream before—but not with all of *you* in it. But is it really you, or am I just dreaming you?"

"You're not dreaming *me,*" Lewis said. "I think I'm dreaming you."

Rob ignored him and shook his head at Kait. "There's no way for me to prove I'm real—not until tomorrow."

Strangely, that convinced Kait. Or maybe it was just the nearness of Rob, the way her pulse quickened when she looked at him, the certainty that her mind couldn't be making up anything this vivid.

"So now we're sharing *dreams?*" she asked edgily.

"It must be the telepathic link. That web of yours," said Anna.

"If Kaitlyn's had the dream before, it's *her* fault," said Lewis. "Isn't it? And where are we, anyway?"

Kaitlyn looked up and down the narrow spit of land. "I don't have a clue. I've only had this dream a couple of times before, and it never lasted this long."

"Can't you dream us somewhere warmer?" Lewis asked, teeth chattering.

Kaitlyn didn't know how. This dream didn't *feel* like a dream exactly—or, rather, she felt much more like the waking Kaitlyn than the fuzzy Kaitlyn who moved semiconsciously through dreams.

Anna, who seemed least affected by the cold, was kneeling near the edge of the water. "This is strange," she said. "You see these piles of stones everywhere?"

It was something Kaitlyn hadn't noticed before. The peninsula was bordered with rocks, most of which looked as if they had just washed up. But some of the rocks were gathered into stacks, piled one on top of another to form whimsical towers. Some rocks had their long axis up and down, some were placed horizontally. Some of the towers looked a bit like buildings or figures.

"Who did it?" Lewis asked, aiming a kick at a pile.

"Hey, don't," Rob said, blocking the kick.

Anna stood up. "He's right," she told Lewis. "Don't spoil things. They're not ours."

*They're not anyone's. This is just a dream,* Gabriel said, throwing a look more chilling than the wind at them.

"If it's *just* a dream, how come you're still in it?" Rob asked.

Gabriel turned away silently.

Kaitlyn knew one thing: This particular dream had gone on *much* longer than any of the others. And they might not really be here, but Rob's skin was covered with gooseflesh. They needed to find shelter.

"There must be somewhere to go," she said. Where the peninsula joined the land, there was a very wet and rocky beach. Above that, a stony bank, and then trees. Tall fir trees that formed a dark and uninviting thicket.

On the other side, water . . . and across the water, a lonely cliff, bare in some places, black with forest in others. There was no sign of human habitation, except—

"What's that?" she said. "That white thing."

She could scarcely make it out in the dimness, but it looked like a white house on the distant cliff. She had no idea how one might get to it.

"It's useless," she murmured, and at the same moment a surge of warmth swept over her. How strange—everything was getting cloudy. She was suddenly aware that while she was standing on the rocky peninsula, she was also lying down . . . lying down in bed. . . .

For a moment it seemed as if she could choose where she wanted to be.

Bed, she thought firmly. That other place is too cold.

And then she was turning over, and she *was* in bed, pulling up the covers. Her brain was too foggy to think of calling to the others, of finding out if it really had been a shared dream. She just wanted to sleep.

The next morning she woke up to: *Oh, no.*

*Lewis?* she thought hazily.

*Hi, Kaitlyn. Hi, Rob.*

*G'way, Lewis. I'm sleeping,* Rob said indistinctly. Only, of course, he didn't say it, not with his voice. He was in his own bedroom, and so was Lewis. Kait could *feel* them there.

She looked up over hummocks of sheets and blankets, to see Anna looking at her from the other bed. Anna looked flushed with sleep, sweet, and resigned.

*Hi, Anna,* Kaitlyn said, feeling somewhat resigned herself.

*Hi, Kait.*

*Hi, Anna,* Lewis said chirpily.

*And good night, John-boy!* Gabriel shouted from across the house. *Shut the hell up, all of you!*

Anna and Kaitlyn shared a look. *He's crabby when he wakes up,* Kaitlyn observed.

*All boys are,* Anna told her serenely. *At least he seems to have got his strength back.*

*I thought,* Rob said, his mental voice seeming more awake, *that you said it would be gone by this morning.*

Thunderous silence from Gabriel.

*We might as well get dressed,* Kaitlyn said at last when the silence went on. *It's almost seven.*

She found that if she concentrated on herself, the others receded into the background—which was just as well, she thought as she showered and dressed. There were some things you *needed* to be alone for.

But no matter what she did, they were there. Lurking around the edges of her mind like friends just within earshot and shouting range. Paying attention to any one of them brought that one closer.

Except Gabriel, who seemed to have locked himself off in a corner. Paying attention to him was like bouncing off the smoothness of his steely walls.

It wasn't until she was dressed that Kaitlyn remembered her dream.

"Anna—last night—did you dream anything in particular?"

Anna looked up from beneath the glistening raven's wing of her dark hair. "You mean about that place by the ocean?" she said, brushing vigorously. She seemed quite undisturbed.

Kaitlyn sat down. "Then it was real. I mean, you were really there." *You guys were all in my dream,* she added silently, so the others could hear it.

*Well, it's not really that surprising, is it?* Rob asked from his room. *If our minds are linked telepathically, and one of us has a dream, maybe the others get dragged in.*

Kaitlyn shook her head. *There's more to it than that,*

she told Rob—but what more, she didn't know. Just then Lewis interrupted anyway, from the stairway.

*Hey, I think Joyce is home! I hear somebody in the kitchen. Come on down!*

All thoughts of the dream vanished. Kaitlyn and Anna ran out and met Rob on their way to the staircase.

"Joyce!" Lewis was saying when they got to the kitchen. He was also saying *Joyce!* but Joyce didn't seem to notice.

"Are you all right?" Kaitlyn asked. Joyce looked very pale, and there were huge dark circles under her eyes. She looked . . . young, somehow, like a kid with a short haircut that's turned out wrong.

Kaitlyn swallowed, but couldn't manage the next words. Anna said them for her. "Is Marisol . . . ?"

Joyce put down a box of Shredded Wheat as if it were heavy. "Marisol is . . . stable." Then her adult control seemed to desert her and she blurted, lips trembling, "She's in a coma."

"Oh, God," Kaitlyn whispered.

"The doctors are watching her. I stayed with her family at the hospital last night, but I didn't get to see her." Joyce fished in her purse, found a tissue, and blew her nose. She picked up the Shredded Wheat box and looked at it blankly.

"Now, you just let go of that and sit down," Rob said gently. "We'll take care of everything."

"That's right," Kaitlyn said, glad for the guidance. She herself felt sick and terrified. But *doing* something made her feel better, and in a few minutes they had Joyce sitting at the kitchen table, with Anna stroking her hand, Kaitlyn making coffee, and Rob and Lewis setting out bowls and spoons.

"It's all so confusing," Joyce said, wiping her eyes and crumpling the tissue in her fist. "Marisol's family didn't know she was on medication. They didn't even know she'd been seeing a psychiatrist. I had to tell them."

Kaitlyn looked at Rob, who, shielded by the pantry door, returned the look with grim significance. Then, carefully measuring scoops of ground coffee, she asked Joyce, "Who told *you* she was seeing a shrink?"

"Who? Mr. Zetes." Joyce passed a hand over her forehead. "By the way, he said you kids behaved really well last night. Went to bed early and all."

Anna smiled. "We're not children." She was the only one who could talk; the others were all engaged in a torrent of silent communication.

*I knew it*, Kaitlyn was telling Rob. *Joyce doesn't know anything about Marisol except what comes from Mr. Z. Don't you remember—when I asked about Marisol's medication, she told me, "He said a psychiatrist prescribed it." It was Mr. Zetes who told her that. For all we know, Marisol wasn't on any medication at all.*

Rob's face was tight. *And now she's in a coma because—*

*Because she knew too much about what was going on here. What was really going on,* Kait finished.

*Which you guys still haven't told us,* Lewis reminded her. *But look, why don't we tell Joyce what's going on? I mean, what's going on with us. She might know how this telepathy thing works—*

*NO!*

168

The thought came like a clap of thunder from upstairs. Kaitlyn involuntarily glanced upward.

Gabriel's mental voice was icily furious. *We can't tell anyone—and especially not Joyce.*

"Why not?" Lewis said. It took Kaitlyn a moment to realize he'd said it aloud. Anna was casting alarmed glances from the table.

"Uh, anybody want sugar or Equal or anything on their cereal?" Rob interjected. *Lewis, be careful!* he added silently.

"Sugar," Lewis said, subdued. *But why can't we tell Joyce? Don't you trust her?* he added in what came across as a mental stage whisper.

"Equal," Kaitlyn said, to Rob. *I do trust her—I think. I don't believe she knows anything—*

*You idiot! You can't trust anyone,* Gabriel snarled from upstairs. The volume of his thoughts was giving Kaitlyn a headache.

Looking pained, Rob and Lewis sat down at the table. Kaitlyn poured Joyce a cup of coffee and joined them. The spoken and unspoken conversations formed an eerie counterpoint to each other.

*I hate to say this, but I think he's right,* Rob said silently, when the echoes of Gabriel's forceful message had died. *I want to trust Joyce, too—but she tells Mr. Zetes everything. She told him about Marisol, and look what happened.*

"Everything's going to be all right," Anna told Joyce. *She's very upset over Marisol. That's genuine,* she told the others.

*She's an adult,* Gabriel said flatly. *You can't trust any adult, ever.*

*And if she's innocent, she could get hurt,* Rob added.

"If there's anything we can do to help Marisol, let us know," Kaitlyn said to Joyce. *All right. We won't tell her,* she conceded. *But we need to get information about telepathy from somewhere. And we need to talk about what Rob and I found in that hidden room.*

Rob nodded, and covered it with a violent spasm of coughing. *We'd better meet at school—alone. Otherwise talking like this is going to drive me crazy.*

Kaitlyn felt agreement from everywhere, except upstairs.

*That means you, too, Gabriel,* Rob said grimly. *You're the one who started this. You're going to be there, boy.*

Aloud he said, "Could somebody pass that orange juice, please?"

# 13

They met at lunch, and Kaitlyn and Rob told about everything they'd found in Mr. Zetes's hidden office below the stairs. Anna and Lewis were as puzzled as Kait had been over the various files and papers.

"Psychoactive weaponry," Gabriel said, seeming to relish the words. By unanimous agreement they were all talking out loud, and Kaitlyn couldn't tell what Gabriel was thinking behind his barriers.

"Do you know what it means?" Rob asked. His attitude toward Gabriel had changed overnight. There was a new tolerance in him—and a new combativeness. Kaitlyn had the slightly alarmed feeling that he meant to push and challenge Gabriel whenever he thought it was good for Gabriel.

"Well, psychoactive should be obvious even to a moron," Gabriel said. "It means something activated by psychics."

*As opposed to something activated by psychos?*

"Lewis!" Kaitlyn, Anna, and Rob all said. Gabriel contented himself with a withering look.

"I couldn't help it. I'm sorry. I'm not saying anything, see?" Lewis took a desperate chug of milk.

"Something . . . activated . . . by psychic power," Gabriel repeated coldly, one eye on Lewis. When there was no interruption, he turned to Rob. "Do I have to explain weaponry, or can you manage that alone?"

Rob leaned forward. "Why . . . would NASA . . . want him . . . to develop weaponry?"

Kaitlyn slammed a fork on the table between them to get their attention. "Maybe NASA didn't want him to actually develop it—but to find out if somebody *else* could be developing it. Eighty-six was the year the *Challenger* shuttlecraft exploded, right? Well, what if NASA thought the explosion was, like, sabotage? *Psychic* sabotage?"

"Sabotage by who?" Rob asked quietly.

"I don't know—the old Soviet Union? Somebody else who didn't want the space program to go ahead? If you got psychics to develop PK that could work over really long distances, you could have them throw switches in the shuttlecraft while they were sitting here on earth. I know it's not a nice idea, but it's possible."

"We're not dealing with nice people," Anna said.

"Look, what about all the other things in that room?" Lewis asked. "The pilot study stuff, and the letter from the judge—"

"Forget it. All of it," Gabriel said sharply, and when several people turned to protest, he added, *Forget it!*

*We've got something else to worry about first. Understand?*

Kaitlyn nodded slowly. "You're right. If this . . . web . . . that connects us gets unstable . . ."

"Even if it doesn't, we've got to get rid of it," Gabriel said brutally. "And the only place to get information about telepathy—*hard* information, in detail—is the Institute."

"That's right, Joyce has a bunch of books and journals and things in the lab," Lewis said. "But she's going to think it's weird that we're suddenly interested."

"Not if we go now," Gabriel said. "She's probably asleep."

"She *might* be asleep," Kaitlyn said cautiously. "And she might not be—and Mr. Zetes might be there. . . ."

"And pigs might fly. We'll never find out unless we go see." Gabriel stood, as if everything were decided.

*Jeez, he's sure active all of a sudden. Now that he's got a stake in things.*

"Lewis," Kaitlyn said mildly. But Lewis was right.

Joyce was asleep, with the French doors to her room wide open. Kaitlyn glanced at Rob, and what otherwise would have been just a meaningful look took on words.

*Too bad,* she told him. *I was hoping we might get a chance to go back into that hidden room—but it's too risky. She'd hear us.*

He nodded. *It would have been too risky anyway. Those doors are mostly glass—and if she woke up, she'd be looking straight out at that panel.*

Lewis was screwing his face into an unaccustomed frown. *I thought we were supposed to be talking out loud.*

*Not when we're standing outside Joyce's door,* Kaitlyn said. *This thing is useful when we need to be quiet.* She moved stealthily away.

They found Gabriel already in the front lab, kneeling by a bookcase, scanning the journals inside. Kaitlyn went to help him.

"There are more bookcases in the back," Anna said, and she and Lewis went through the door. Rob joined Kaitlyn. He didn't need to say anything—she could feel his watchful protectiveness. He meant to keep an eye on her when Gabriel was around.

*There's no need,* Kaitlyn thought, and then wondered if anyone had heard her. Oh, she didn't *like* this—this *exposure*. Not being sure if your own thoughts were private. She reached crossly for a book.

*We've got to get rid of this thing.*

On either side of her, Rob and Gabriel were radiating agreement.

They looked for what seemed like hours. Kaitlyn scanned journals with names like *Journal of the American Society for Psychical Research* and *Research in Parapsychology.* Some were translations of foreign journals with tongue-twisting names like *Sdelovaci Technika.*

There were articles about telepathy, thought projection, suggestibility. But nothing that looked remotely helpful to their situation.

At last, when Kaitlyn was beginning to worry that Joyce *had* to wake up soon, Anna called excitedly from the other room.

*People, I've found something!*

They all hurried to the back lab and gathered around her.

"'On stability in telepathic linkage as a function of equilibrium in self-sustaining geometric constructs,'" she said, holding a journal with a red cover. "It's about groups in telepathic links—groups like *us.*"

"What on earth is a self-sustaining geometric construct?" Kaitlyn asked, very calmly.

Anna flashed a smile. "It's a web. You said it yourself, Kaitlyn—we're like five points that are joined to form a geometrical shape. And the point is that it's *stable*—that's what this article is saying. Two minds connected aren't stable. Three or four minds connected aren't stable. But five minds connected are. They form a—a sort of stable shape, and the whole thing stays in balance after that. That's why we're still linked."

Rob glanced at Gabriel. "So it's your fault. You shouldn't have connected all five of us."

Gabriel ignored him, reaching for the journal. "What I want to know is how to get *un*connected."

"I'm getting there," Anna said, holding it away from him. "I haven't read that part yet, but it's got a section here about how to disrupt the stability and break the connection." Her eyes scanned down the page as she continued to hold the journal away from Gabriel.

The others waited impatiently.

"This says that it's all theoretical, that nobody's ever really gotten five minds linked together. . . . Wait . . . then it says that some *larger* groups may be stable, too. . . . Okay, here. Got it." Anna began to read aloud. "'Breaking the link would be harder than initiating it, would require a far greater amount of power. . . .' But wait, it says there *is* one certain way of breaking it—" Anna stopped abruptly, eyes fixed on the page. Kaitlyn could feel her shock and dismay.

"What?" Gabriel demanded. "What does it say?"

Anna looked up at him. "It says the only certain way of breaking the connection is for one of the group to die."

Everyone stared at her, stunned. There was no sound, either mental or vocal.

"You mean," Lewis said shakily, at last, "that the web won't kill us—but that the only way to get rid of it is for one of us to *be* killed?"

Anna shook her head—not a negative, merely a helpless gesture. "That's what the article says. But—it's only a theory. Nobody can really know—"

Gabriel snatched the journal from her. He read rapidly, then stood for a moment very still. Then, with a furious gesture, he threw the journal at a wall.

"It's permanent," he said flatly, turning to stare at the wall himself.

Kaitlyn shivered. His anger frightened her, and it mixed with her own feelings of shock and fear.

In a lot of ways she'd enjoyed the connection. It was interesting, exciting. Different. But to *never* be able to break it . . . to know you'd be stuck in a web until one of them died . . .

My whole life has changed, she thought. Forever. Something . . . irrevocable . . . has happened, and there's no way to undo it.

I will never be alone, unconnected, again.

"At least we know it's not going to kill any of us," Anna said in a quiet voice.

Kaitlyn said slowly, "Like you said, that article might be wrong. There might be some other way to break it—we can read other books, other journals, and see."

"There is a way. There *has* to be," Gabriel said, in a cracked, almost unrecognizable voice.

He's the most desperate of all of us, Kait realized with something like dispassion. He can't stand being this close—having us all this close to him.

*Until we find it, you all stay away from me,* Gabriel's mental voice said, as if in answer to Kaitlyn's thought. Had he heard her?

"Meanwhile," Rob said in a quiet, level voice, "we might work on learning how to control it—"

*Just stay away!* Gabriel shouted, and he strode out of the room.

Lewis, Anna, Rob, and Kaitlyn were left staring after him.

"Why's he so mad at *us?*" Lewis asked. "If it's anyone's fault, it's his."

Rob smiled faintly. "That's why he's mad," he said in a dry voice. "He doesn't like being wrong."

"It's more than that," Kaitlyn said. "He helped us—and look where it got him. So it just confirms what he thought in the first place, that you should never help."

There was another silence, while everyone just stood. We still haven't taken it all in, Kaitlyn thought. We're in shock.

Then she gave herself a mental shake. "Those

bookcases look pretty bad. We'd better clean things up quick. We can look for other articles about breaking the web later, when we know Joyce won't be around."

They straightened the books and the rows of plastic journal holders in both labs. It was as she was putting on the final touches that Kaitlyn found another article that intrigued her.

Someone had marked the page with a red plastic Post-it flag. The title was simply "Chi and Crystals."

*You guys? What's chi?* she asked, scarcely aware that she wasn't asking it out loud.

"It's a Chinese word for your life energy," Lewis said, coming to her. "It flows all through your body in different channels, sort of like blood—or electricity. Everybody has it, and psychics have more of it."

"So chi is what Rob channels?" Kaitlyn said.

"That's one name for it," Rob said. "At the other center they told me lots of others—like in India they call it *prana,* and the ancient Egyptians used to call it *sekhem.* It's all the same thing. All living things have it."

"Well, according to this article, crystals store it," Kaitlyn said.

Rob frowned. "Crystals aren't alive. . . ."

"I know, but this says that theoretically a crystalline structure could store it up, kind of like a charged battery," Kaitlyn said. She was still looking at the article thoughtfully. Something was tugging at her, whispering significance, demanding that she pay attention to it. But she didn't know *what.*

The article looked as if it had been read a lot. . . .

"She's up," Rob said. Kaitlyn could hear it, too—

water running in the single downstairs bathroom. Joyce was awake and washing.

Anna checked her watch. *It's three-thirty. We can just tell her that we walked home from school.*

Kaitlyn nodded and she felt agreement from the others. She straightened her back, kept her head high, and went to face Joyce.

The week that followed was hectic. There was school to go to during the days, and testing with Joyce in the afternoons. Any leisure time was filled with two things: trying to find a way to break the web, and trying to find out more about Mr. Zetes's plans. The problem was that they didn't make much progress with either.

They didn't get into the hidden room again. Although Kait and Rob waited for a chance, Joyce never left the Institute again and she slept with her doors open.

Kaitlyn lived in a perpetual state of astonishment and nervousness. It was hard to be constantly on her guard with Joyce, to keep from talking about the only two things that were now important in her life. But somehow she managed it—they all managed it.

Marisol remained in a coma. No one outside her family was allowed to visit her, but Joyce called every day. Every day the news was the same: no change.

Mr. Zetes visited the Institute several times, always unexpectedly. They kept their secrets from him, too— or at least, Kaitlyn was pretty sure they did. Occasionally, when she saw Mr. Z's penetrating dark eyes lingering on Gabriel, she wondered.

Gabriel himself was . . . disturbing. Disturbed. Not taking things well.

For Kaitlyn, even though this new intimacy was strange and terrifying, it was exciting, too. She'd never been so close to other people in her life. The sparkling enthusiasm of Lewis's thoughts—the cool serenity of Anna's—that was *good.* And the closeness to Rob was almost painful delight.

But for Gabriel, it was all torture. He spent every minute of his free time reading journals and books, trying to find a way to break the web. He convinced Joyce he was simply interested in researching his talent, and she was delighted. She let him go to the library and get more books, more journals.

He didn't find anything helpful. And every day he didn't, he withdrew further from the others. He learned how to wall himself off telepathically so that Kaitlyn could barely sense his presence.

*We're trying to leave you alone,* she told him. And it was true, they were, because they were all worried. Gabriel seemed to be getting wound tighter and tighter, like something waiting to explode.

On Tuesday, one week after the web was established, Joyce tested Kaitlyn with the EEG machine again.

Kaitlyn had been waiting for this. *I think she's going to do it,* she told Rob. They had gotten pretty good at sending messages to specific people.

*I can come in any time you want,* he said. *But what do you want me to do—just try to watch her?*

Kaitlyn debated as she followed Joyce's instructions to sit down and close her eyes. *No—if there's anything she doesn't want you to see, she won't let you watch. Could you make a distraction when I tell you to? It only needs to last a minute.*

*Yes,* Rob said simply.

Now that Marisol wasn't there to help, Joyce had stopped testing Gabriel at all, and usually sent Rob and a volunteer to the back lab while the other three did their testing in the front. Rob was there now with Fawn, the girl who had MS. Kaitlyn could feel him waiting, alert and vigilant.

"Right; you know how to do this," Joyce said, sticking a final electrode in place—in the center of Kaitlyn's forehead. Over her third eye. "I'll concentrate on the picture. You relax."

Kait murmured something, concentrating on the feel of that single electrode. Cold. It was definitely colder than all the others, and her forehead had a prickling feeling.

When she relaxed, letting her mind fall into darkness, she knew what to expect.

It came. First the feeling of incredible pressure behind her forehead. It turned into a feeling of inflation, like a balloon being blown up. Then came the pictures.

They flashed through her mind with bewildering speed, and she could only recognize a few. She saw roses and a horse. She saw Mr. Zetes in front of the hidden doorway again. She saw a white house with a caramel-colored face in the window.

And—unexpectedly—she heard voices.

Anna's voice: *Kait—I can't think—what's happening?*

Lewis's: *Jeeeeeeeez.*

Rob's: *Just hang on, everybody.*

At the same time, to Kait's astonishment, she could clearly hear Gabriel. *What the hell is this? What are you trying to do?*

She forced herself to ignore the distracting pictures. *Gabriel, where are you?*

*Just coming up on Exmoor Street.*

Kaitlyn was amazed. Exmoor Street was blocks away from the Institute. They'd found that their telepathy fell off sharply with distance, and anything more than a block was too far for clear communication.

But Gabriel was clear now—painfully clear.

*I'll explain later,* Kait told him. *Just try to deal with it for a few minutes.* Then she told Rob, *Now.*

Immediately she heard a thud, and then Fawn's voice shouting. "Joyce! Oh, please—Rob's hurt!"

Kaitlyn remained perfectly still, eyes shut. She heard a rustle on the other side of the screen, then Anna's voice saying, *She's going. She's in the back lab now.*

Kaitlyn opened her eyes, reaching up to her forehead. The little electrode came away easily, but something remained behind. She could feel it with her fingertips, something stuck to her skin by the electrode cream.

Carefully, her heart beating violently, she peeled it off.

When she looked at it, pinched between thumb and forefinger, she got a shock of disappointment. It wasn't anything after all—just a lump of white electrode cream. Then her fingernails scraped at it and she saw that beneath the coating of paste was something hard. It was white, too, or translucent, which made it difficult to see. It was about the size and shape of her little fingernail, and quite smooth and flat.

It looked like crystal.

All this time she could hear faint voices in the other room. Now Rob said, *Watch out, Joyce is standing up.*

Quickly Kaitlyn stuck the small crystal back onto her forehead. She jammed the electrode on over it, praying they both would stay.

*She's coming back,* Lewis reported.

*Here she is,* Anna said.

Kait rubbed the telltale paste from her fingers onto her jeans. She picked up the pencil and clipboard and began to draw. It didn't matter what. She sketched a rose.

The folding screen was moved. "Kaitlyn, I'm going to unhook you," Joyce said in a rapid, harassed voice. "Rob's completely collapsed—I think he's overdone things with that girl. Anna, Lewis, can you help get him to the couch here? I want him to lie down for a while."

Kaitlyn held still, fingers curled because she was guiltily aware that there was still electrode cream under her fingernails. She was relieved that Joyce didn't seem to notice anything peculiar about the forehead electrode. What *Kaitlyn* noticed, though, was that after taking that one off, Joyce's hand went quickly to her shirt pocket. As if palming something and putting it away.

*Rob, you okay?* Kaitlyn asked, as Lewis and Anna helped him in, and Joyce turned to settle him on the couch.

She got the mental impression of a wink. *Just fine. Did you see anything?*

*A crystal,* Kait told him. *We need to talk about this, try to figure it all out.*

Rob said, *Sure thing. Just as soon as she lets me get up.*

"Before you go, what did you draw?" Joyce asked, looking up as Kait headed for the door.

Kaitlyn got the clipboard and showed her the rose picture.

"Oh, well—better luck next time. It was supposed to be a horse. I'm sorry we had to interrupt your testing."

"It doesn't matter," Kaitlyn said. "I'm going upstairs to get this electrode stuff out of my hair." Silently she added, *We'd better meet before dinner.*

She went upstairs. She wanted to think, but somehow her head seemed cloudy, her thoughts slow.

Rob's voice came to her. *Kaitlyn—are you feeling okay?*

Kaitlyn started to answer, and then *realized* just how she was feeling. *Oh, Rob, I'm stupid. I forgot what happened to me last time she did this.*

She could sense revelation and sympathy from Lewis and Anna, but Rob put it into words. *A headache.*

*A bad one,* Kaitlyn admitted. *It's coming on fast and getting worse.*

Rob's frustration was almost palpable. *And I'm stuck down here with Joyce fussing over me.*

*It doesn't matter,* Kait told him quickly. *You're supposed to be in a collapse, so stay collapsed. Don't do anything to make her suspicious.*

To distract herself, she looked out the window,

squinting against the mild light. And then she saw something that made her heart jump into her throat.

Instantly there was an answering wave of alarm from downstairs. *What, what?* Lewis said. *What's wrong?*

*It's nothing,* Kaitlyn said. *Don't worry. I've just got to check something out.* It was the first time she'd tried to deceive the others, but she wanted a moment to think alone. She pulled away from them mentally, knowing they'd respect that. It was like turning your back in a crowded room: the only kind of privacy any of them had now.

She hesitated by the window, looking out at the black limousine parked on the narrow dirt road—and the two figures beside it. One was tall, white-haired, wearing a greatcoat. The other lithe, dark-haired, wearing a red pullover.

Mr. Zetes and Gabriel. Talking in a place where no one could hear them.

# 14

Kaitlyn hurried downstairs and slipped out the back door.

Quietly, she told herself as she made her way down the hill behind the Institute. Quietly and carefully. She kept to the blurred shadows of the redwood trees, creeping up on her prey.

She got close enough that she could hear Gabriel and Mr. Zetes talking. She knelt behind a bush, looking at them cautiously through the prickly wintergreen foliage.

It gave her a grim satisfaction to realize that Gabriel's wall-building could have some drawbacks. He'd barricaded himself from the rest of them so efficiently that he didn't sense her a few yards away. Fortunately, Mr. Zetes's dogs didn't seem to be around to spot her, either.

Shamelessly eavesdropping, Kaitlyn strained her ears.

One dread pounded inside her, sharper than her

headache. She had a terrible fear that they were talking about the web.

In a way, she wouldn't be surprised. The strain on Gabriel had been growing every day. He was desperate, and desperate people look for desperate cures.

But if he'd betrayed them, if he'd gone to Mr. Zetes behind their backs . . .

As she listened, though, her heartbeat calmed a little. It didn't seem to be that kind of conversation. Mr. Zetes seemed to be stroking Gabriel's ego, complimenting Gabriel in a vague and extravagant way. Like somebody buttering up a fraternity pledge, Kaitlyn thought. It reminded her of the speech Mr. Zetes had given the first day at the Institute.

"I know how you must feel," he was saying. "Repressed, hemmed in by society—forced into this *ordinariness*. This *mediocrity.*" Mr. Zetes gestured around him, and Kaitlyn instinctively scrunched lower behind her bush. "While all the time your spirit feels caged."

That's nasty, Kaitlyn thought. Talking about cages to someone just out of a boys' prison . . . that's *low*.

"Alienated. Alone," Mr. Zetes continued, and Kait allowed herself a grin. She knew for a fact that one thing Gabriel was *not* feeling these days was alone.

Mr. Zetes seemed to sense that he was off the mark, too, because he went back to harping on the repressed and caged bit. He was manipulating Gabriel; that was clear enough. But why? Kaitlyn thought. She could barely feel Rob, Lewis, and Anna from here, and she didn't dare try to get in touch with them. It would certainly alert Gabriel, and she wanted to find out what was going on.

"Society itself will someday realize the injustice that's been done to you. It will realize that extraordinary people must be allowed a certain liberty, a certain freedom. They must follow their own paths, without being caged by laws made for ordinary individuals."

Kaitlyn didn't like the expression on Gabriel's face, or the dim feelings she could sense from him behind his walls. He looked . . . *smug,* self-important. As if he were taking all this crap seriously.

It's the strain, Kaitlyn thought. He's so sick of us that he's gone right round the bend.

"I think we should continue this discussion at my house," Mr. Zetes was saying now. "Why don't you come up with me this evening? There's so much we have to talk about."

Horrified, Kaitlyn saw that Gabriel was shrugging. Accepting. "I've been wanting to get away," he said. "In fact, I'd do just about anything to get out of here."

"We might as well go from here," Mr. Zetes said. "I was going to pay a visit to the Institute, but I'm sure Joyce can carry on without me."

Alarm flashed down Kaitlyn's nerves and her heart thumped. Gabriel was getting in the car. They were going to leave right *now*—and there was no time to do anything.

Only one thing. She stood up, trying to look bold and casual at once, and to think clearly despite the pain in her head.

"Take me, too," she said.

Two heads snapped around to look at her. Gabriel had paused with one foot inside the limousine. Both he and Mr. Zetes looked very startled, but in an instant Mr. Zetes's expression had changed to fierce, pitiless scrutiny.

"I've been listening," Kaitlyn said, since this was obvious. "I just came down to—to think, and I saw you, and I listened."

Gabriel's eyes were dark with fury—he was taking it as another invasion of his privacy. "You little—"

"Different rules for extraordinary people," Kaitlyn told him imperiously, standing her ground. "Society shouldn't cage me in." It was the best she could do trying to remember the gibberish Mr. Z had been spouting.

And it seemed to soften Mr. Z's fierce expression. His grim old lips curved a little. "So you agree with that," he said.

"I agree with freedom," Kaitlyn said. "There're times when I feel just like a bird hitting a pane of glass—and then flying back a little and hitting it again—because I just want to get *out.*"

It was the truth, in a way. She *had* felt like that— back in Ohio. And the ring of truth seemed to convince Mr. Zetes.

"I often thought you might be the second one to come around," he murmured, as if to himself. Then he looked back at her.

"I should very much like to talk to you, my dear," he said, and there was a tone of formality, of *finality*, in his voice. As if the simple words were part of some ceremony. "And I'm sure Gabriel will be delighted to have you along."

He made a courteous gesture toward the limo.

Gabriel was gazing at Kaitlyn darkly, looking unconvinced and not at all delighted to have her. But as she slowly got into the car, he shrugged coldly. "Oh, sure."

"Shouldn't we go to the Institute first?" Kaitlyn asked, as Mr. Zetes got in and the limousine began to move, backing up smoothly toward the bridge. "I could change my clothes. . . ."

"Oh, you'll find things quite informal at my home," Mr. Zetes said, and smiled.

They were getting farther away from the purple house every second. *Rob*, Kaitlyn thought, and then with more force. *Rob! Rob!*

She got only a distant sense of mental activity as an answer. Like hearing a muffled voice, but being totally unable to make out the words.

*Gabriel, help me,* she thought, deliberately turning her face away, looking out the limousine window. It frightened her to be using telepathy with Mr. Zetes in the car, but she didn't have a choice. She sent the thought directly at Gabriel, jarring through his walls. *We need to tell Rob and the others where we're going.*

Gabriel's response was maddeningly indifferent. *Why?*

*Because we're going off with a nut who could have anything in mind for us, that's why! Don't you remember Marisol? Now, just help me! I can't get through to them!*

Again Gabriel seemed completely unaffected by her urgency. *If he were going to put us in a coma like Marisol, he would hardly need to take us to San Francisco,* he said contemptuously. *And besides, it's too late now. We're too far away.*

He was right. Kaitlyn glared out the window, trying not to let her tension show in her body.

*Nobody asked you to come and invite yourself along,* Gabriel told her, and she could feel the genuine coldness behind his words. The resentment and anger. *If you don't like it, that's your own fault.*

He hates me, Kaitlyn thought bleakly, putting up walls of her own. She wasn't as good at it as he was, but she tried. Right now, she didn't want to share anything with him.

It was getting dark, the swift chilly darkness of a winter evening. And every mile the limousine went north was taking her farther and farther away from Rob and the Institute, and closer to she didn't know what.

By the time they reached San Francisco, it was fully dark, and the city lights twinkled and gleamed in skyscraper shapes. The city seemed vaguely menacing to Kaitlyn—maybe because it was so beautiful, so charming and cheerful-looking. As if it were decked out for a holiday. She felt there had to be something beneath that lovely, smiling facade.

They didn't stay in the city. The limo headed toward dark hills decorated with strings of white jewels. Kaitlyn was surprised at how quickly the tall buildings were left behind, at how soon they were passing streets of quiet houses. And then the houses began to be farther and farther apart. They were driving through trees, with only an occasional light to show a human habitation.

The limousine turned up a private driveway.

"Nice little shack," Gabriel said as they pulled up in

front of a mansion. Kaitlyn didn't like his voice at all. It was mocking, but dry and conspiratorial, as if Mr. Zetes would appreciate the joke. As if Gabriel and Mr. Zetes shared something.

Something *I* don't share, Kaitlyn thought. But she tried to put the same tone in her own voice. "Really nice."

Under heavy eyelids, Gabriel gave her a glance of derisive scorn.

"That's all for tonight," Mr. Zetes told the chauffeur as they got out. "You can go home."

It gave Kaitlyn a tearing sensation to watch the limousine cruise away. Not that she'd ever said more than "hello" to the driver, but he was her last connection with . . . well, normal human beings. She was alone now, with Mr. Zetes and a Gabriel who seemed to resent her very existence.

"I live very simply, you see," Mr. Zetes was saying, walking up the columned path to the front door. "No servants, not even the chauffeur. But I manage."

Prince and Baron, the two rottweilers, came bounding up as he opened the door. They calmed at a glance from Mr. Zetes, but followed closely behind him as he and his visitors walked through the house. Just another thing to make Kaitlyn nervous and unhappy.

Mr. Zetes took off his coat and hung it on a stand. Underneath he was wearing an immaculate, rather old-fashioned suit. With real gold cuff links, Kait thought.

The inside of the house was as impressive as the outside. Marble and glass. Thick, velvety carpets and polished, gleaming wood. Cathedral ceilings. All sorts of foreign and obviously expensive carvings and vases. Kaitlyn supposed they were art, but she found some of them repulsive.

Gabriel was looking around him with a certain expression—one it took her a moment to categorize. It was . . . it was the way he'd been looking at the magazine with the expensive cars. Not greedy; greed was too loose and unformed. This expression had *purpose;* it was sharp and focused.

Acquisitive, Kaitlyn thought. That was it. As if he's planning to *acquire* all this. As if he's determined to.

Mr. Zetes was smiling.

I should look like that, too, Kaitlyn thought, and she tried to stamp an expression of narrow-eyed longing on her own face. All she wanted was to fool Mr. Zetes until he let them go home. At the beginning she'd had some idea about finding things out about Mr. Zetes—but not anymore. Now she was just hoping to live through whatever was coming and get back to the Institute.

"This is my study," Mr. Zetes said, ushering them into a room deep in the large house. "I spend a great deal of time here. Why don't you sit down?"

The study was walnut-paneled and darkly furnished, with leather chairs that creaked when you sat on them. On the walls were gold-framed pictures of horses and what looked like fox hunts. The curtains were a deep, lightless red, and the lamps all had rust-colored shades. There was a bust of some old-fashioned-looking man on the mantelpiece and a black statue of a foreign-looking woman on the floor.

Kaitlyn didn't like any of it.

But Gabriel did, she could tell. He leaned back in his chair, looking around appreciatively. It must be a guy thing, Kaitlyn thought. This whole place is so masculine, and so . . . Again, she had trouble finding a word. The closest she could come was *old money*.

She supposed she could see why Gabriel, used to living on the road or in a cell with one bunk and a metal toilet, might like that.

The dogs lay down on the floor. Mr. Zetes went over to the bar—there was a full bar, with bottles and silver trays and crystal decanters—and began pouring something. "May I offer you a brandy?"

My God, Kaitlyn thought.

Gabriel smiled. "Sure."

*Gabriel!* Kaitlyn said. Gabriel ignored her completely, as if she were a fly buzzing around the perimeter of the room.

"Nothing for me, thanks," she said, trying not to sound as frightened as she felt. Mr. Zetes was coming back with only two glasses, anyway—she didn't think he'd even meant to include her in the offer.

He sat down behind the desk and sipped golden liquid out of a ballooning glass. Gabriel sat back in his chair and did the same. Kaitlyn began to feel like a butterfly in a spider's web.

Mr. Zetes himself seemed more aristocratic and imposing than ever, more like an earl. Someone important, someone who ought to be listened to. This whole study was designed to convey that impression, Kaitlyn realized. It was a sort of shrine that drew your attention to the figure behind the large, carved desk. The figure with the immaculate suit and the real gold cuff links and the benevolent white head.

The atmosphere was beginning to get to her, she realized.

194

"I'm so glad we're able to have this talk," Mr. Zetes said, and his voice went with the atmosphere. It was both soothing and authoritative. The voice of a man who Knew Best. "I could see right away at the Institute that you were the two with the most potential. I knew that you'd outstrip the others very quickly. You both have so much more capacity for understanding, so much more sophistication."

Sophisticated? Me? Kaitlyn thought. But a part of her, a tiny part, was flattered. She'd been more sophisticated than other kids in Thoroughfare, she knew that. Because while all they'd been thinking about was cheerleading or football games, she'd been thinking about the world. About how to get out into the world.

"You can conceive of . . . shall we say, broader horizons," Mr. Zetes was saying, as if he'd followed her train of thought. It was enough to bring Kait up short, to make her look at him in alarm. But his piercing old eyes were smiling, bland, and he was going on. "You are people of vision, like myself," he said. He smiled.

"Like myself."

Something in the repetition make Kaitlyn very nervous.

It's coming, she realized. Whatever it is. He's been building up to something, and here it is.

There was a long silence in the room. Mr. Zetes was gazing at his desk, smiling faintly, as if lost in thought. Gabriel was sipping his drink, eyes narrowed but on the floor. He seemed lost in thought, too. Kaitlyn was too uneasy to speak or move. Her heart had begun a slow, relentless hammering.

The silence had begun to be terrible, when Gabriel raised his head. He looked Mr. Zetes in the eyes, smiled faintly, and said, "And just what is your vision?"

Mr. Zetes glanced toward Kaitlyn—a mere formality. He seemed to assume that Gabriel spoke for both of them.

When he started talking again, it was in a dreadful tone of complicity. As if they *all* shared a secret. As if some agreement had already been reached.

"The scholarship is only the beginning, of course. But naturally you realize that already. The two of you have such . . . enormous potential . . . that with the right training, you could set your own price."

Again Gabriel gave that faint smile. "And the right training is . . . ?"

"I think it's time to show you that." He put his empty glass down. "Come with me."

He stood and turned to the walnut-paneled wall of the study. As he reached out to touch it, Kaitlyn threw Gabriel a startled glance—but he wasn't looking at her. His entire attention seemed fixed on Mr. Zetes.

The panel slid back. Kaitlyn saw a black rectangle for one instant, and then a reddish glow flicked on as if activated automatically. Mr. Zetes's form was silhouetted against it.

My picture! Kaitlyn thought.

It wasn't, exactly. Mr. Zetes wasn't wearing a coat, for one thing, and the red light wasn't as bright. Her picture had been more a symbol than an actual rendition—but she recognized it anyway.

"Right this way," Mr. Zetes said, turning to them almost with a flourish. He expected them to be surprised, undoubtedly, but Kaitlyn couldn't work herself up to pretending. And when Gabriel entered the gaping rectangle and started down the stairway, she realized she couldn't protest, either. It was too late for that. Mr. Zetes was looking at her, and the dogs were on their feet and right behind her.

She had no choice. She followed Gabriel.

This stairway was longer than the one at the Institute, and it led to a hallway with many doors and several branching corridors. A whole underground complex, Kaitlyn realized. Mr. Zetes was taking them to the very end.

"This is . . . a very special room," he told them, pausing before a set of double doors. "Few people have seen it. I want you to see it now."

He opened one of the doors, then turned toward them and stopped where he was, gesturing them in, watching their faces. In the greenish fluorescent light of the hallway his skin took on an unhealthy chalky tone and his eyes seemed to glitter.

Kaitlyn's flesh began to creep. She knew, suddenly and without question, that whatever was in there was terrible.

Gabriel was going in. Mr. Zetes was watching her with those glittering eyes in a corpselike face.

She didn't have a choice.

The room was startling in its whiteness. All Kaitlyn could think at first was that it was exactly what she'd imagined the laboratories at the Institute would be like. White walls, white tile, everything gleaming and immaculate and sterile. Lots of unfamiliar machinery around the edges, including one huge metal-mesh cage.

But that was all incidental. Once Kaitlyn was able to focus on anything, she focused on the thing in the center of the room—and then she forgot everything else.

It was . . . what? A stone plant? A sculpture? A model spaceship? She didn't know, but she couldn't look away from it. It drew the eye inevitably and then held it fast, the way some very beautiful paintings do—except that it wasn't beautiful. It was hideous.

And it reminded Kaitlyn of something.

It was towering, milky, semitranslucent—and that should have given her a clue. But she couldn't get over her first impression that it was some horrible parody of a plant, even when she realized that it couldn't be.

It was covered with—things. Parasites, Kait thought wildly. Then all at once she realized that they were growths, smaller crystals sprouting from a giant parent. They stuck out in all directions like the rays of a star, or some giant Christmas decoration. But the effect wasn't festive—it was somehow obscene.

"Oh, God—what *is* it?" Kaitlyn whispered.

Mr. Zetes smiled.

"You feel its power," he said approvingly. "Good. You're quite correct; it can be terrible. But it also can be very useful."

He walked over to the . . . thing . . . and stood beside it, the dogs padding at his heels. When he looked at it, Kaitlyn saw that his eyes were admiring—and acquisitive.

"It's a very ancient crystal," he said, "and if I told you where it came from, you wouldn't believe me. But it will amaze you, I promise. It can provide energy beyond anything you've ever imagined."

"This is the training you were talking about?" Gabriel asked.

"This is the means of training," Mr. Zetes said softly, almost absently. He was still looking at the crystal. "The means of sharpening your powers, increasing them. It has to be done gradually to avoid damage, but we have time."

"*That* thing can increase our powers?" Gabriel said with scorn and disbelief.

"Crystals can store psychic energy," Kaitlyn said in a small voice. It sounded small and distant even to her. She had the feeling of someone who'd walked into a nightmare.

Mr. Zetes was looking at her. "You know that?" he said.

"I . . . heard it somewhere."

He nodded, but his eyes lingered on her as he said, "You two have the potential—this crystal has the power to develop that potential. And I have . . ." He stopped, as if thinking how to phrase something.

"What do you have?" Gabriel said.

Mr. Zetes smiled. "The contacts," he replied. "The . . . clients, if you will. I can find people who are willing to pay considerable amounts for your services. Amounts that will climb as your powers are honed, of course."

Clients, Kaitlyn thought. That letter—the letter from Judge Baldwin. A list of potential clients.

"You want to hire us out?" she blurted before she could stop herself. "Like—like—" She was too overwrought to think of an analogy.

Gabriel could think of one. "Like assassins," he suggested. His voice chilled Kaitlyn—because it wasn't at all outraged or indignant. He sounded quite calm—thoughtful, even.

"Not at all," Mr. Zetes said. "I think there would be very few assassinations involved. But there are a number of business situations in which your talents would be invaluable. Corporate espionage—industrial sabotage—influence of witnesses at certain trials. No, I would prefer to call you a psychic strike team, available for handling all sorts of situations."

A strike team. Project Black Lightning, Kaitlyn thought. The words scribbled on that piece of paper. He wanted to turn them into a paranormal dirty tricks team.

"I hadn't meant to explain all this to you so quickly," Mr. Zetes was going on. "But the truth is that something has come up. You remember Marisol Diaz, of course. Well, there has been a bit of a problem with Marisol's family. Several of them have become . . . unexpectedly difficult. Suspicious. I'm afraid that money has little influence on them. I need to quiet them some other way."

There was a pause. Kaitlyn couldn't say anything because she felt as if she were choking, and Gabriel simply looked sardonic.

"I thought we weren't assassins," he said.

Mr. Zetes looked pained. "I don't need them killed. Just quieted. If you can do it some other way, I'm very happy."

Kaitlyn managed to get words through the blockage in her throat. "You did it to Marisol," she said. "You put her in the coma."

"I had to," Mr. Zetes said. "She had become quite

unstable. Thank you for bringing that to my attention, incidentally—if you hadn't mentioned it to Joyce, I wouldn't have realized so soon. Marisol had been with me for several years, and I thought she understood what we were doing."

"The pilot study," Kaitlyn said.

"Yes, she told you about that, didn't she? It was a very great pity. I didn't know then that only the strongest minds, the most gifted psychics, could stand contact with one of the great crystals. I gathered six of the best I could find locally—but it was a terrible disaster. Afterward I realized that I would have to expand my search—cover the whole nation—if I wanted to find students who could tolerate the training."

"But what happened to *them?*" Kaitlyn burst out. "To the ones in the pilot study—"

"Oh, it was a dreadful waste," Mr. Zetes said, as if repeating something she should have gotten the first time. "Very good minds, some of them. Genuine talent. To see that reduced to idiocy and madness is very sad."

Kaitlyn couldn't answer. The hair on her arms and the back of her neck was standing up. Tears had sprung to her eyes.

"Marisol, now—I did think she understood, but in the end she proved otherwise. She was a good worker in the beginning. The problem was that she knew too much to be simply bribed, and she was too temperamental to be controlled by fear. I really had no other choice." He sighed. "My real mistake was to use drugs instead of the crystal. I thought a seizure might be very effective—but instead of dying, she wound up in the hospital, and now her family is posing a problem. It's really very difficult."

He might look like an earl—but he was insane, Kaitlyn thought. Truly insane, insane enough that he didn't realize how insane all this would sound to sane people. She looked at Gabriel—and felt a shock that sent chills up from her feet.

# 15

Because Gabriel didn't look as if he found it insane. Slightly distasteful, maybe, but not crazy. In fact, there was something like agreement in his face, as if Mr. Z were talking about doing something unpleasant but necessary.

"But we can take care of that problem," Mr. Zetes said, looking up and speaking more briskly. "And once it's over, we can get to our real work. Always assuming you're interested, of course?"

His voice had a note of gentle inquiry, and he looked from Gabriel to Kaitlyn, waiting for an answer. Again Kaitlyn felt a shock of disbelief. Those dark, piercing eyes of his looked so acute—how could he not realize what she was feeling? How could he look at her as if he expected agreement?

She had exploded into speech before she knew what was happening. All the fear, all the fury, all the disgust and horror, that had been building inside her burst out.

"You're *insane*," she said. "You're completely insane, don't you know that? Everything that you've said is completely *insane*. How can you talk about people being reduced to idiots as if—as if—" She was degenerating into sobs and incoherence. "And *Marisol*," she gasped. "How could you do that to *her*? And what you want to turn us all into—you're just completely, totally *crazy*. You're *evil*."

She was having hysterics, she supposed. Raving. Shouting as if shouting were going to do any good. But she couldn't stop herself.

Mr. Zetes seemed less surprised than she did. Displeased, certainly, but not astonished. "Evil?" he said, frowning. "I'm afraid that's a very emotional and inexact word. Many things seem evil that are, in a higher sense, good."

"You don't *have* any higher sense," Kaitlyn shouted. "You don't care about anything except what you can get out of us."

Mr. Zetes was shaking his head. "I'm afraid I can't waste time in arguing now—but I honestly hope you'll see reason eventually. I think you will, in time, if I keep you here long enough." He turned to Gabriel. "Now—"

Then Kaitlyn did something she realized was stupid even as she was doing it. But her anger at Mr. Zetes's insufferable smugness, his indifference to her words, drove her beyond any caution.

"You won't get any of the others to join you," she said. "Not any of them back home. Rob wouldn't even *listen* to it. And if I don't come back, they'll know something's wrong. They already know about the hidden room there at the Institute. And they're linked, we're all linked telepathically. All five of us. And—"

"*What?*" Mr. Zetes said. For the first time, a real emotion was showing on his face. Astonishment—and anger. He looked at Gabriel sharply. "What?"

"We are, aren't we?" Kaitlyn demanded. "Tell him, Gabriel." *And tell him he's crazy, because you know he is. You know he is!*

"It's something that happened," Gabriel told Mr. Zetes. "It was an accident. I didn't know it would become permanent. If I had"—he glanced at Kaitlyn—"it never *would* have happened."

"But this is— You're telling me that the five of you are involved in a stable telepathic link? But don't you realize . . . ?" Mr. Zetes broke off. There was plenty of emotion in his face now, Kaitlyn noted. It was dark with blood and fury. "Don't you realize that you're useless within a linked group like that?"

Gabriel said nothing. Through their connection, Kaitlyn could feel that he was as angry as Mr. Zetes.

"I was counting on you," Mr. Zetes said. "I *need* you to help me take care of the Diaz problem. If that isn't controlled . . ." He stopped. Kaitlyn could see he was making a great effort to get hold of himself. And, after a moment or two, he apparently succeeded. He sighed, and the fury drained out of his face.

"There's no help for it now," he said. "It's a very great pity. You don't know how much work is wasted." He looked at Kaitlyn. "I had great hopes for you."

Then he said, "Prince, back."

Kaitlyn had almost forgotten about the dogs—but now one came straight for her, hair bristling, teeth showing to the gums. It was completely silent, which only made it scarier.

Involuntarily Kaitlyn took a step backward—and the dog kept coming. As it reached her, she stepped back again and again—and then she realized what was happening. She was standing inside the metal cage.

Mr. Zetes had gone over to a kind of console across the room. He pressed a button and the door to the cage slid shut.

"I told you," Kaitlyn said tensely. "If you keep me here, they'll know—"

Mr. Zetes interrupted as if he didn't notice her speaking. Turning to Gabriel, he said, "Kill her."

Shock washed over Kaitlyn like an icy bath—and again and again. She'd realized, all at once, just *how* stupid she'd been. The cold reality of her situation left her unable to breathe. Unable to think.

"Don't worry; it's just a Faraday cage," Mr. Zetes was telling Gabriel. "It's built to keep out normal electromagnetic waves, but it's quite transparent to your power. It's like the steel room at the Institute, and you projected easily through that."

Gabriel was silent. His stony expression told Kaitlyn nothing, and she couldn't feel anything from him through the web. Maybe she was just numb.

"Go on," Mr. Zetes said. He was beginning to look impatient. "Believe me, there's no other alternative. If there were, I would save myself the work of getting another subject like her—but there's no choice. The link has to be broken. The only way to break it is to kill one of the five of you."

Gabriel's chest rose and fell with a sudden deep breath. "The link has to be broken," he repeated, grimly. Kaitlyn did feel something then. She felt that he meant it.

"Then go on," Mr. Zetes said. "It's unfortunate, but it has to be done. It's not as if it's the first time you've killed." He glanced at Kaitlyn. "Have you heard about that? Drains his victims' life energy dry. An extraordinary power." There was a kind of macabre satisfaction in his face.

Then it turned to impatience again. "Gabriel, you know what the rewards will be with me. You can literally have anything you want, in time. Money, power—your rightful position in the world. But you must cooperate. You must prove yourself."

Gabriel stood like a statue. Except for that one sentence, he hadn't said a word. Something artistic in Kaitlyn's brain watched him with mad clarity, thinking about how really beautiful his face was in repose. He looked a bit like his namesake, like an angel carved in white marble. Except for his eyes, which were definitely not an angel's eyes. They were dark and fathomless—and right now rather pitiless. Cold as a black hole.

One could very easily imagine an assassin having eyes like that.

Then something like sadness entered them. Because he's sorry to have to kill me? Kaitlyn wondered.

She felt nothing at all through the telepathic web. It was like being connected to a glacier.

"Go on," Mr. Zetes said.

Gabriel glanced at Kaitlyn, then at the white-haired man.

"I'd rather kill you," he said conversationally, to Mr. Zetes.

Kaitlyn didn't get it at first. She thought he might just be stating a preference, rather than refusing.

Mr. Zetes, though, looked unamused. Forbidding. He put one hand behind him.

"If you're not for me, you're against me, Gabriel," he said. "If you won't cooperate, I'll have to treat you as an enemy yourself."

"I don't think you'll have time," Gabriel said, and took a step toward him.

Kaitlyn grabbed at the metal mesh of her cage. Her numbed brain was finally getting things together. She wanted to laugh hysterically—but it didn't seem right.

*Don't kill him,* she thought wildly to Gabriel. *Don't really kill him—he's crazy, don't you see? And we've got to do things—police, an institution—but we can't actually* kill *people.*

Gabriel tossed her the briefest of glances. *"You're* the one who's crazy," he said. "If anybody ever deserved it, it's him. Not that your idea didn't have its points," he added to Mr. Zetes. "Especially in the rewards department."

Mr. Zetes's eyes shifted from Kaitlyn to Gabriel during this exchange. They narrowed, and he nodded slightly.

Kaitlyn was waiting for some sign of fear. It didn't come. Mr. Zetes seemed calm, even resigned.

"You won't change your mind?" he asked Gabriel.

Gabriel took another step toward him. "Good night," he said.

Mr. Zetes brought his hand from behind his back, and Kaitlyn saw that he was holding a dark and very modern, very nasty-looking gun.

"Baron, Prince—guard," he said. And then he added, "If you make a move now, these dogs will jump up and tear out your throat. And then there's the gun—I've always been a very good shot. Do you think you can dispose of all three of us with a knife before we can kill you?"

Gabriel laughed—a very disquieting sound. Although his back was to Kaitlyn now, she knew that he was giving Mr. Zetes his most dazzling, disturbing smile. "I don't need a knife," he said.

Mr. Zetes shook his head, gently and disparagingly. "There's something I'm afraid you haven't realized. Joyce hasn't tested you since you formed this . . . unfortunate linkage, has she?"

"So what?"

"If she had, you would have discovered by now that it's quite difficult for a telepath who is already in a stable link to reach outside that link. Nearly impossible, I believe. In other words, young man, except for communications within your group of five, you've lost your power."

Kait could feel the disbelief surging in Gabriel. His walls were lowered now, his attention was focused elsewhere. Then she felt something like the drawing back of the ocean just before a tsunami—a sort of gathering in Gabriel's mind. She braced herself—and felt him unleash it.

Or try to. The wave, instead of crashing down on

Mr. Zetes, seemed to crash around her and Gabriel instead.

It was true. He couldn't link with anyone else. Not to communicate with them—and not to harm them.

"And now, if you'll sit down in that chair," Mr. Zetes said.

Kaitlyn's eyes shifted to the chair. She'd barely noticed it before. It stood on the opposite side of the room from the door, and it looked frighteningly high-tech. It was made of metal.

With the gun in front of him and a dog on either side, Gabriel backed up to the chair. He sat.

Mr. Zetes went over and made some quick movements, stooping once. When he stood, Kaitlyn realized that Gabriel was now restrained in the chair by metal cuffs at his wrists and ankles.

Then Mr. Zetes stepped behind the chair. Two winglike devices swung forward. In another instant, Gabriel's head was held motionless by a device that looked as if it were meant for brain surgery.

"The crystal can do more than just amplify power," Mr. Zetes said. "It can cause excruciating pain—even madness. Of course, that was what happened with the pilot study." He stepped back. "Are you quite comfortable?" he asked.

Kaitlyn was remembering the pain that had resulted from being in contact with a tiny shard of the crystal, a piece the size of her fingernail.

Mr. Zetes went over to the towering thing with the jagged growths in the center of the room. For the first time, Kaitlyn realized that the metal stand that supported it was mobile. The entire structure, though obviously heavy, could be moved.

Very carefully and delicately, Mr. Zetes was bringing the crystal to Gabriel. Tipping it slightly. Adjusting it. Until one of the jagged terminals, one of the growths, was resting against Gabriel's forehead.

In direct contact with the third eye.

"It will take a while for it to build. Now I'm going to leave the room," Mr. Zetes said. "In an hour or so I'll come back—and by then I think you might have changed your mind."

He walked out. The dogs went with him.

Kaitlyn was alone with Gabriel—but there was absolutely nothing she could do.

She looked wildly at the door of the metal cage, pulled at it with the strength of desperation. She only succeeded in cutting her fingers. It took her about two minutes to discover that there was no way she could affect it, with fists or feet or the weight of her body.

"Don't bother," Gabriel said. The strain in his voice frightened her into going over to look at him.

He was completely immobile, his face white as paper. And now that Kaitlyn was still, she could feel his pain through the web.

He was trying to hold it back, to close himself—and the pain—off from her. But even what little got through to her was terrible.

The pressure behind the forehead—like what she had experienced with the crystal Joyce had used, but indescribably worse. As if something alive were swelling there, trying to get out. And the heat—like a blowtorch directed against that spot. And the sheer black agony—

Kaitlyn's knees gave out. She found herself half lying on the floor of the cage.

Then she pulled herself up to a sitting position.

*Oh, Gabriel* . . .

*Leave me alone.*

"I'm sorry," she whispered, saying it and sending it at once. *I'm so sorry. . . .*

*Just leave me alone! I don't need you. . . .*

Kaitlyn couldn't leave him alone. She was locked into it with him, sharing the waves of agony that kept building. She could feel them break over her, spread out infinitely around her. Spreading, swelling . . . to include all of them. All five who shared the web.

*Kaitlyn!* a distant voice shouted.

The connection was shaky, tenuous. But Kaitlyn recognized Rob.

It wasn't just pain. It was power. The crystal was feeding Gabriel power.

*Rob—can you hear me? Lewis, Anna—can you hear me?*

*Kaitlyn, what's happening? Where* are *you?*

*It's them, Gabriel! We've got them! It's them!* For a minute, despite the screaming of her nerves, Kaitlyn was simply delirious with joy.

*We might lose them any second,* Gabriel said. But Kaitlyn could feel what he felt—there were no walls between them now. The crystal had annihilated those. And his relief and joy were as strong as hers.

*Rob, we're in Mr. Zetes's house. You've got to find out somehow where that is—and fast.* Kaitlyn told them about the study, and the panel. *It might be closed again, but Lewis can open it. But you have to hurry, Rob—come quick.*

*If you want to find us alive,* Gabriel added. Kaitlyn was amazed that he was even speaking coherently. She

212

knew that he was taking the worst of the pain himself.
She felt a surge of admiration for him.

*Keep it to yourself, witch,* he told her.

It was an endearment, she realized. Witch. She
supposed she'd better learn to like it.

*You could have told Mr. Zetes you'd think about
killing me. You could have bought yourself time,* she
said.

*I don't bargain with people like him.*

Kaitlyn, through the waves of pain that were start-
ing to be tinged with crimson and carmine, felt an
intense pride and triumph. *You see?* she thought to
Rob. *Mr. Zetes was wrong about all of us. You see how
wrong?*

But Rob wasn't there anymore. The connection had
been too fragile—or now the pain was wiping everything out.

She leaned against the metal cage, dimly feeling its
coolness. *Hang on,* she thought. *Hang on. Hang on.
He's coming.*

She didn't know if she was saying it to Gabriel or to
herself, but he answered. *You believe that?*

It roused her a little. *Of course,* she said. *I know he
is. And so do you.*

*It's dangerous. He's risking his own neck by coming
here,* Gabriel said.

*You know he's coming,* Kaitlyn said, able to say it
with perfect assurance because she could *feel* it,
directly.

"Rob the Virtuous," Gabriel said, aloud. He made
a contemptuous sound like a snort—which was
marred because he almost immediately gasped in
pain.

Kaitlyn could never really remember the time that passed after that. It wasn't time to her, so much as a series of terrible, endless waves that eventually turned brilliant, bursting red and white like molten rock. She had no means of keeping track of them, and no consciousness of anything but them. She was alone with the waves of colored agony, thrown about by them like a swimmer caught in a riptide.

Alone—except for Gabriel. He was there, always connected. They were both being thrown around by the pain, dimly aware of each other. Kaitlyn didn't think it did Gabriel much good to know she was there, but she was glad of his presence.

It seemed a very long time, centuries maybe, but at last she sensed another presence in the maelstrom that was her world.

*Kaitlyn—Gabriel. Can you hear us now? Kaitlyn! Gabriel!*

*Rob.* Her own response was so weak and faltering, so small in the huge waves, that she didn't think he would hear it.

*Thank God! Kait, we're here. We're in the house. Everything is going to be all right—Joyce is with us. She's on our side. She didn't know anything about what he was doing. We're coming to help you, Kait.*

There was a near frenzy to Rob's words. Emotion— an emotion Kait had never sensed from him before. But she couldn't think now. Too much pain.

She lost awareness until she felt a presence very close.

Rob. She dragged herself up. The room was both too bright and strangely gray and dim. Alternating, like lightning. Rob was there, golden as an avenging angel, somehow coming between her and the pain. And Lewis was there, and Anna, both crying. And Joyce, her sleek blond hair all ruffled like a dandelion. They were running toward the crystal, although Kaitlyn saw their movements as discontinuous, as if under a strobe lamp.

And then—like a light switch being turned off—the pain was gone.

It left echoes, of course, and normally Kaitlyn would have found even the echoes unbearable. But it was so different from the actual pain that she felt wonderful. Able to think again, able to breathe. Able to see.

She saw that Joyce had pulled the terminal of the crystal away from Gabriel. His forehead was bleeding freely, the skin torn. He must have moved his head somehow, in spite of the metal restraints. The blood ran down his face in streams, as if he were crying.

He'd hate that, Kaitlyn thought. But Gabriel wasn't awake to be hating it. She realized now that it was some time since she'd felt any sort of communication from him, even a scream. He was unconscious.

The door of the Faraday cage was opening. Rob was beside her. Rob was holding her.

*Are you all right? Oh, God, Kait, I thought I might lose you.*

There it was again. The new emotion. The one that felt almost like pain, but was different.

Kaitlyn looked up into Rob's eyes.

*I didn't know,* he said. *I didn't realize how much I had to lose.*

It was like being transported back to the afternoon when he'd looked at her with awe and wonder, on the brink of a discovery that would change both their lives. Except that now he wasn't just on the brink. The full discovery was in those golden eyes, shining with terrible clarity. A pure light that was almost impossible to look at.

*It would have been like losing me, like losing my own soul,* Rob said, but it wasn't really like him saying it to her, it was as if he were simply realizing these things himself. *And now it's like finding my soul again. The other half of me.*

Kaitlyn felt it again, the universe around her hushed and waiting, enclosing the two of them. This time, though, there was a trembling joy to the hush, a *certainty.* They weren't on the threshold anymore. They were passing through. Everything being said between them, without spoken words or even words of the mind. It was simply as if their souls were mingling, joining in an embrace that wasn't quite the web and wasn't quite Rob's healing power, although it had elements of both.

It was beyond all that. It was a union, a *togetherness,* that Kaitlyn had never dreamed of.

*I'm with you. I belong to you.*

*I'm a part of you. I will be forever.*

Kaitlyn didn't even know which of them was speaking. The feelings were in both of them.

*We were born for this.*

He was holding her hands, she was holding his. She could feel the power flowing between them, the energy like millions of sparkling lights, like fresh, cleansing water, like music, like stars. But she felt she was healing him as much as he was healing her. Giving him back what the accident had taken from him, the part of him that had been missing.

And then it was all so simple and natural. As if they both knew what to do without thinking—as if they'd always known what to do.

She tilted her face up, he bent down.

His lips touched hers.

In a minute they were exchanging the softest, most innocent kisses imaginable.

Kait had *never* thought that kissing a boy would be like this.

Not even Rob. She'd thought that kissing Rob would be wonderful. But this wasn't like something physical at all. It was simply like falling into the color of Rob's eyes. It was like falling endlessly into sunlight and gold.

*Born for each other. For this.*

A long sunlit wave, a wave of gold, came and carried them away.

Dimly, gradually, Kaitlyn was aware of a loud sound. A loud *vocal* sound.

"I said, I'm sorry to interrupt you, but really. Rob, there's something to do here!"

It was Joyce, sounding sadly unmusical after the lovely voices Kaitlyn had been hearing. Joyce was looking at them, impatient and worried, and the tears on Anna's face were still wet. It had only been a minute or so since they'd all come in.

Impossible, of course. Kaitlyn in her heart knew it had been hours, but that was *real* time, soul time, and not the time that was ticking away on this dreary planet. She and Rob had been floating around for hours, but it had only taken a minute *here*.

Rob disengaged himself, letting go of Kaitlyn's hands. A small parting, but a hard one. Kaitlyn's fingers curled, empty.

"I'm sorry. I think I can help Gabriel," Rob said. He got up, took a step, then turned back to Kait. He knelt down by her again. *I forgot to say, I love you.*

Kaitlyn gave a half-gasping laugh. As if *that* needed to be said. "You go help Gabriel," she whispered.

"No, I need both of you," Joyce was saying. "And *quickly.* You can't solve this with energy channeling, Rob—he needs to be brought back from wherever he is. I need all four of you to get in contact with the crystal."

That broke through the lingering gold haze in Kaitlyn's vision. *"What?"* she said, standing up. She noticed dimly that she felt good, physically. Strong. Healing power *had* flowed between her and Rob.

"I need you all to get in contact with the crystal," Joyce said patiently. "And Gabriel, too—"

"No!"

"It's the only way, Kaitlyn."

"You saw what it did!"

"This time it will only be for a moment. But I need *all* of you to touch the crystal, everyone who's in the link. Now, for God's sake, hurry. Don't you realize that Mr. Zetes may be back at any minute?"

Kaitlyn staggered as she made her way out of the cage. To let the crystal touch Gabriel again— impossible. It couldn't be done, it was too cruel. And the crystal was *evil;* Kaitlyn knew that. . . .

But Joyce said it was the only way.

Kaitlyn looked at Joyce, who looked back with clear aquamarine eyes. Eyes that looked anguished but earnest.

"Don't you want to save him, Kait?"

Kaitlyn's hand began to itch and cramp.

She needed to draw—but there wasn't any time. No time. And nothing to draw with. Not a pen or paper in this entire sterile lab.

*"Please* trust me, everyone. Come on, Lewis. Just get your hand ready to touch it. When I say *now,* grab a terminal."

Lewis took a deep breath and then nodded. He held his hand ready.

"Anna? Good. Thank you. Rob?"

Rob looked at Kaitlyn.

If she could draw . . . But she couldn't. Looking back at Rob, Kaitlyn made a helpless motion that ended with a nod.

"We'd better do it," she whispered.

Joyce shut her eyes and sighed in relief. "Good. Now, I'll get behind Gabriel. When I say *now,* I'll move him in contact. Each of you grab a terminal and hold on, right?"

Kaitlyn could vaguely sense the others agreeing. She herself was moving to stand in front of the crystal, one hand outstretched. But her mind was whirring with frantic speed.

I can't draw . . . not with my hands. But the power's not in my hands. It's in my head, in my mind. If I could draw in my mind . . .

# 16

Even as Kaitlyn thought it, she was doing it. Desperately visualizing oil pastels, her favorite, sweeps of color. First I'd take lemon yellow, fluffy sweeps, with dashes of palest ocher. Then curves of flesh tint—and two small pools of light blue and Veronese green, dotted together.

All right! What is it? Step back! Step back and look.

In her mind, she stepped back, and the sweeps and dots made a picture. Joyce. Unmistakably Joyce.

Then gray. Curves and lines of gray. A shape—a glass. With flesh tones holding it—Joyce holding a glass.

"Everyone ready?" Joyce said.

Kaitlyn didn't move, didn't open her eyes. She was concentrating on the next part of the picture. Rich olive-hued flesh, with a mass of burnt umber and deep madder for hair. The brown and red went together to make mahogany.

Marisol. A picture of Joyce and Marisol. And Joyce was holding out to Marisol a glass—

"I've got his head," Joyce said. "And—*now*—"

Kaitlyn's scream, both mental and verbal, cut through the words. *"Don't do it! Don't do it! She's with him—Mr. Zetes!"*

In the split second that followed, she wondered if she might be wrong. Joyce might have given Marisol something unknowingly—but the picture hadn't said that. It might not even be a picture of a real event, but for once, the *meaning* was clear to Kaitlyn. And the meaning was one of menace and danger. It felt to her the way the picture of the old witch giving Snow White a poisoned apple had felt to Kaitlyn the child.

And, even as Kaitlyn opened her eyes, she saw that she *hadn't* been wrong. Joyce had thrust Gabriel's head against the crystal and was holding it, and her face had an expression that Kaitlyn had never seen before. A look of twisted, bestial fury.

*She knew all the time. She was in on everything,* Kaitlyn thought, sickened. She could feel the shock and pain of the others—especially Rob. But her shout had reached them in time. Not one of them had touched the crystal.

Except Gabriel—Gabriel, who was now being roused from unconsciousness by the white-hot lightning bolts of pain.

Kaitlyn started to move—to tear Joyce away from Gabriel. Rob started at the same moment she did. But before they could get there, the doors burst open and chaos exploded on them.

It was Mr. Zetes—and the dogs. Something

knocked into Kaitlyn with the force of a speeding truck and she fell. A dog was ripping at her. Mr. Zetes had the gun.

Still holding Gabriel against the crystal, Joyce was shouting. "I'll break the link! I'll break it!"

Rob was fighting the other dog. Anna was trying to pull the animal off him, her own calls to it lost in the clamor.

"There's an easier way to break it! Only one of them needs to die!" Mr. Zetes shouted. He was aiming the gun at Lewis.

And this is how it ends, a part of Kaitlyn's mind thought, curiously detached. None of them could help Lewis. None of them could do anything before Mr. Zetes could shoot.

She seemed to sense the old man's finger tightening on the trigger. At the same time she saw the room as one large picture, every detail etching itself into her mind as if with the burst of a flashbulb. Rob and Anna tangled with the rottweiler, Lewis standing in almost comical horror, Joyce's twisted face over the face of Gabriel, whose cheeks were masked in blood and who was just opening his eyes . . .

She felt Gabriel's awakening at the same instant, felt his pain—and his fury. Someone was hurting him. Someone was threatening a member of his web.

Gabriel lashed out.

Mr. Zetes had said that a telepath in a stable link couldn't reach outside that link—but Gabriel was now connected to a source of unthinkable power. His mind blazed out like the flare of a supernova—in four directions. With absolute precision and deadly force, he sent a torrent of fire through Mr. Zetes and Joyce and the two dogs.

Kaitlyn felt the dim shadows of it through the web, the reverberations of what Gabriel had unleashed on them. It knocked her flat.

Mr. Zetes fell without firing a shot. Behind Gabriel, Joyce hit the wall. The dog tearing Kaitlyn's arm spasmed as if it had been electrocuted and was still.

Then Gabriel stopped it. He had sagged back from the crystal, collapsing. The entire room was silent and motionless.

*Let's get out of here,* Rob gasped.

Kaitlyn was never sure how they got out of the house. Rob was the main force in moving them. He practically carried Gabriel. She and Anna and Lewis helped each other. There was a long time of stumbling and dragging and finally they were on grass.

Grass cool with dew. It felt wonderful. Kaitlyn rested against it gratefully, as if she'd just staggered out of a fire.

At last Lewis whispered thickly, "Are they dead?"

*The dogs are, I think,* Anna said. Kaitlyn agreed, but didn't mention that she'd seen blood coming out the eyes and nose and ears of the one on top of her.

*But Mr. Zetes and Joyce—I don't know,* Anna finished. *I think they might be alive.*

"And so Joyce didn't want to save Gabriel," Lewis said.

"She wanted to break the web somehow," Kaitlyn said, not surprised to find her voice hoarse. "Even if it killed us. Gabriel wasn't any good to them linked to us. . . . Don't ask why. I'll explain everything later."

"But Joyce was bad," Lewis said sadly. The simple innocence of the statement caught Kait—and did something to her.

Joyce was bad. She'd been against them, ready to use them, the whole time. Marisol had been wrong; Joyce had clearly known everything. She'd known about the big crystal and had had no hesitation about using it. She must have known all about the hidden room, too.

"God," Kaitlyn whispered. "How could I have been so dumb? It was probably *her* room—everything was copies, remember, Rob? Duplicates. Mr. Zetes had his stuff here, and she had hers in the Institute."

"Kaitlyn," Rob whispered, and there was both pain and tenderness in his voice, although he couldn't reach her since he was cradling Gabriel. "Don't. It's not worth it."

Kaitlyn looked at him in surprise—and realized she was crying. Thick streams of tears. She put a hand to her cheek and touched the wetness. As soon as she did, she felt something swell up in her chest.

And then she was sobbing, huge sobs, the kind she hadn't cried since she was eight years old.

Anna held her. *Leave her alone,* she told Rob. *She deserves to cry. We all do.*

The shaking sobs passed quickly, and Kaitlyn began to feel better.

Gabriel was stirring.

"This time," Rob told him, "you don't have any choice. You're half-dead—and we can't stay here. You *have* to take help." He added, silently, where it would mean more, *You saved my life a little while ago. There's only one way I can repay that.*

Gabriel blinked. He looked terrible—the blood and the pain had distorted his handsome face. But he managed a trace of the old arrogance as he whispered, "Only because I can't stop you."

Kaitlyn stopped sniffling and smiled. *It's not much good to talk like that when all your walls are down,* she told him. Then she added, *I like you this way. Walls can be very bad things.*

Gabriel ignored her, which was all he could do at the moment.

Now Rob was touching Gabriel with gentle, irresistible fingers, and Kaitlyn could feel strength flowing into Gabriel. Through Rob's healing points, through the telepathic web. She put her hand on Rob's and added her own strength, letting Rob take her energy and channel it into Gabriel. Lewis and Anna crowded close and touched Rob's hand, too, adding their contribution. All four of them, linked tightly, willing life and energy into Gabriel.

Kaitlyn could sense his need and his fear—which rapidly turned into astonishment. He'd never felt energy freely given before, she realized. Now she knew what he was feeling and she could feel it with him— the sparkling lights, the pure water, the refreshment. The awakening from half-sleep into real, vivid life.

She could feel astonishment and joy from Anna and Lewis, too.

*And I never believed them about kundalini rising,* Lewis said. *Jeeeez, was I wrong.*

*About what?* Anna asked, laughing in her mind.

*Kundalini—old Chinese health concept. Relating to chi, you know. Remind me to tell you about it sometime.*

Anna, still laughing, said, *I will.*

When they were all feeling ready to ride tigers and fight elephants bare-handed, Rob lifted his hands.

"That's enough," he said, and then added gently, "We really shouldn't stay here. I think Anna was right, and that Joyce and Mr. Zetes are alive. We need to keep moving."

"But where?" Kaitlyn said. She could stand, she found; she could even move easily.

Gabriel was on his feet, too. "Well, out of San Francisco for a start," he said, wiping his face with his dew-wet shirt. Even in the simple act of standing up he had pulled away from them all a little, mentally.

It's only to be expected, Kaitlyn told herself. Don't be disappointed. He needs his space.

"Well, of course, out of San Francisco. But then— where? Home?"

Even as she said it, she knew she couldn't go. If Mr. Zetes and Joyce survived, they would come after her. Kaitlyn knew about them now—Kaitlyn was a danger in the way that Marisol had been a danger. They'd want to have Kaitlyn . . . quieted.

And as much as Kaitlyn adored her father, she knew him very well. He was loving, impractical—vague. Happiest in his own small world, singing and doing odd jobs. What protection could he offer her? He wouldn't even be able to understand her story, much less help her deal with it.

In fact, she'd probably be putting *him* in danger by going home. Nothing would be easier than for Joyce and Mr. Zetes to find her there. And once they found her, she'd be dead—along with anyone else who had heard her story.

Kaitlyn didn't have the least doubt that Mr. Zetes had ways to get people killed. He had contacts. He had clients. He would find a way.

Looking around at the others, she could see them reaching the same conclusion about their own families. She could feel their dawning bewilderment.

"But then . . . where do we go?" Lewis said, in a croaking whisper.

"We have to do something to stop them. Not just Mr. Zetes and Joyce, but whoever else is involved. There must be others—like that judge. We have to find a way to stop them all."

Kaitlyn felt her breath snatched away. She looked at Rob. Yes, she loved him, but really . . . really, she'd just been thinking about how to keep herself and her friends safe. That was going to be hard enough.

"If we don't stop them," Rob said, turning and looking directly at her, "then they'll do it again. They'll try again, with some other group of kids."

Rob was counting on her. Trusting her. And of course, he was right.

"It's true," Kaitlyn said quietly. "We can't let that happen."

"I agree," Anna chimed in softly.

There was a pause, and then Lewis said, "Oh, jeez . . . Count me in."

They all looked at Gabriel.

"I don't even have a home," he said mockingly. "All I know is that I'm not going back into a lockup cell."

"Then come with us," Rob said.

"You don't even know where you're going."

Kaitlyn said, "I might."

Everyone looked quickly at her.

"It's just an idea," she said. "I don't even know exactly why it's come into my head . . . but do you remember that dream, the one we were all in together?"

There were nods.

"Well, what if . . . what if the place in the dream was a real place? When I think about it, I get this sort of feeling that it might be. Does anybody else?"

Everyone looked doubtful, except Anna, who looked thoughtful.

"You know," she said, "I had the same feeling while I was there—in the dream, I mean. That beach felt real. It was a lot like the beaches where I live, up North. It felt almost . . . familiar. And that white house—"

"Wait," Kaitlyn said. "The house. The white house." Her brain was whirring again. She'd seen a white house somewhere else. In her mind this afternoon—could it only be this afternoon?—when Joyce had tested her with the shard of crystal.

She'd never drawn that picture—it had disappeared in a flash. But now she suddenly felt she might be able to reach it again.

Don't think—draw. Draw with your mind. Let your mind go.

Whether it was the recent contact with the great crystal, or simply desperation, she'd never know. But her mind began to draw, sketching with easy, fluid strokes. Vigorous clean strokes. She didn't even have to think about what colors to use. They simply appeared before her, shimmering, in a picture that was completed in a few heartbeats.

A white house, yes. With red roses growing at the door. A lonely house, but an eerily beautiful one. And a face in the window—a caramel-colored face, with slanting eyes and softly curling brown hair.

The man who'd attacked her—but *had* he attacked her? He'd grabbed her and tried to talk with her when she was waiting to meet Joyce. He'd grabbed her in the backyard of the Institute—and she'd hit him. And then he'd called her reckless and told her she never *thought*.

She was thinking now. Whoever he was, he had been in the house in her dream. And he had showed her a picture of a rose garden, with a crystal in the fountain.

She hadn't recognized it as a crystal then. But when she'd seen the big crystal, that monstrosity that Mr. Zetes had owned, she'd almost remembered.

The crystal in the rose garden hadn't looked . . . perverted. It had been clean and clear, with no obscene growths sprouting out. It had looked . . . pure.

So what did it all add up to? Kaitlyn didn't know, but she took a deep breath and tried to explain it to the others.

When she was done, there was a silence.

"So we're following our dreams," Gabriel said with mock sentimentality, his lip still slightly curled.

The words pleased Kait somehow. "Yes," she said, and smiled at him. "And we'll see where they take us."

"Wherever it is, we're going together," Rob said.

Kaitlyn looked at him. She was cold and battered

and she knew that the danger was just beginning. And they had no clear idea of which way to travel and even less idea of *how* to travel.

But somehow it didn't matter. They were all alive, and all together. And when she looked into Rob's golden eyes, she knew that it was going to be all right.

# About the Author

LISA JANE SMITH started writing in elementary school and has never been able to break the habit. She wrote her first published book while attending the University of California at Santa Barbara, after which she went on to teach public school for several years. She still likes to encourage young writers to express themselves.

While she makes no claim to psychic powers, she is firmly convinced that streetlights go off at night when she passes. The author of such trilogies as The Forbidden Game, she likes writing about the supernatural because it's a great forum for the battle between good and evil.

She lives in the Bay Area of Northern California where the Dark Visions trilogy is set.

Look for the next exciting book in the
DARK VISIONS trilogy


**VOLUME II: THE POSSESSION**


Kaitlyn's group is on the run; and Mr. Zetes is on their trail. The five psychics hope to find answers in a white house on a distant cliff—but the journey itself may be deadly. And Gabriel now has a terrifying secret . . . he has become a psychic vampire. Can Rob and Kaitlyn save him or will he be claimed by the dark?